PRAISE FOR JOHN SKIPP
AND DON'T PUS...

"Startlingly honest, refreshingly ...ting, unsettling. His best yet."

—Josh ....an, author of *Bird Box*

"John Skipp has never, ever been afraid to walk in the dark: he knows that's where all light shines hardest. Walk with him, trust his vision and his voice. Push the button." -

—Kathe Koja, author of *The Cipher*

"A genie of fire-eating brilliance. In his virtuoso trove, *Don't Push the Button*, John Skipp's X-Acto gaze slays artifice, heals with true, golden heart. No fathom can resist his maestro dives."

—Richard Christian Matheson, author of *Dystopia*

"*Don't Push the Button* is a beautiful, bluesy, angry, affectionate howl of a book. It wants to tear you apart to show you what's wonderful deep inside of all of us. A wild, unpredictable portrait of a bright, burning mind, it showcases Skipp's radical range, dark-hearted humor, and enormous empathy. There's a grace and honesty to these stories that moved me, and made me grateful that John Skipp will always choose to push those buttons."

—Jeremy Robert Johnson, author of *Entropy In Bloom*

"*Don't Push the Button* proves John Skipp doesn't know how to quit, and thank God he doesn't because we're all better for it. An electric collection that showcases the passion, strain, grief, and im-pulses of what it means to be human. These stories get dirty. They get political. They get uncomfortable. Sometimes they just make you laugh. And all the while they shine through with John Skipp's acid-god light and his love for us all, even at our worst. Even when we push his buttons."

—Autumn Christian, author of *Girl Like a Bomb*

"As writers age, we refine our craft to compensate for a creeping disengagement with the world outside our heads. John Skipp has been working against that curve all his life, tearing down fusty literary conventions and bringing the raw realness with a wrecking ball. *Don't Push the Button* hits with the urgency of a ransom note and the hard-won wisdom of a prizefighter's face. To see so unflinchingly into the dark corners of life and still give a shit is less a gift than a miracle, but Skipp wraps that gift in his own skin and he's giving it to you. Open it!"

—Cody Goodfellow, author of ***Unamerica***

"John Skipp is still splatterpunk, knocking your teeth out to a hard and heavy beat. But he's also a goddamn hippie trying to levitate the Pentagon with the power of his words and as you read him, sometimes you could swear it's working. In the war to keep our hearts alive in this heart-breaking world, *Don't Push the Button* is the essential treatise of our pal in the trenches."

—Laura Lee Bahr, author of ***Haunt***

MORE PRAISE FOR JOHN SKIPP AND DON'T PUSH THE BUTTON: AN OPEN LETTER FROM LUCKY McKEE

Skipp and I have danced in the same horror crowd for a couple decades now. We have many mutuals. We've been at the same dinners, parties, random events. Even have our names on the same anthology flick. Though we've never been day-to-day close, I've always liked Skipp tons and respected the hell out of him for all he's brought to the creative world. His warmth, his humor, his way with words? Special. And by that I mean his work and his VIBE. For a legend in the Splatterpunk field, he's a helluva sweet fella.

So when he reached out to me with his new short story collection, asking for a read and a maybe a quote, I thought "Skipp's always had them GOOD kinda vibes. I'm honored and touched he thought of me, so: hell yes."

Welp, I gobbled up all a' them words and oh what an experience it was. Great writers let you all the way into their personal lives, their minds, their souls. They aren't afraid to write down (and make public) SOOOO many things most of us are too chickenshit to say out loud. Skipp hits that sweet spot over and over again in this collection and he does it from so many surprising angles it's downright head-spinning.

When I put down DON'T PUSH THE BUTTON the first thing that crossed my mind wasn't "Hmm. Now for that jazzy quote that might end up on the book jacket." No. My first thought was "This guy and I need to be REAL friends. Not just clink-a-glass-at-a-Hollywood-wank-off- dinner or random-digital-hellos-every-five-years-to-pat-backs when we see or read each other's stuff out in the wild. That's stuff's good, too - and I'm sure we both have a healthy enough of a supply of it considering how long we've both been doing this. No. Skipp's writing is so good, so insightful, so honest, gross, trippy and what-the-fucky, it makes you feel the dearest of friends has suddenly opened their heart ALL the way up to you and you alone. So this is it, this is my quote:

"John Skipp's DON'T PUSH THE BUTTON is so full of rage, humor, truth, wisdom and beauty it makes me want to be one of his REAL friends."

And coming from a beleaguered, self-imposed Hollywood outcast, believe me when I say: I mean it. FUCKING BEAUTIFUL, SKIPP.

—Lucky McKee, writer/director of *May,* co-author (with Jack Ketchum) of *I Am Sam*

OTHER BOOKS BY JOHN SKIPP

Fiction:
THE LIGHT AT THE END*
THE CLEANUP*
THE SCREAM*
DEAD LINES*
THE BRIDGE*
ANIMALS*
THE EMERALD BURRITO OF OZ**
CONSCIENCE
THE LONG LAST CALL
THE LAST GODDAM HOLLYWOOD MOVIE***
JAKE'S WAKE***
SPORE***
THE ART OF HORRIBLE PEOPLE

Non-fiction:
STUPOGRAPHY
THE BIZARRO ENCYCLOPEDIA OF FILM (VOL. I)****

Screenplays:
SICK CHICK FLICKS

Anthologies:
BOOK OF THE DEAD*
STILL DEAD*
MONDO ZOMBIE
THE MAGAZINE OF BIZARRO FICTION (Issue Four)
ZOMBIES
WEREWOLVES AND SHAPESHIFTERS
DEMONS:
PSYCHOS

Novelizations:
FRIGHT NIGHT*

* with Craig Spector
** with Marc Levinthal
*** with Cody Goodfellow
**** with Heather Drain

CL◄SH

Published by CLASH Books in the United States of America.

www.clashbooks.com

Cover and interior design by Matthew Revert

www.matthewrevert.com

Author photo by Susie Juntarakawe

DON'T PUSH THE
BUTTON

New York Times bestselling author
JOHN SKIPP

For all my friends:
past, present, and future.

TABLE OF CONTENTS

INTRODUCTION BY JOSH MALERMAN

John Skipp is a man of many moments. Great moments. Beats in the history of letters that ripple wider than the genre, wider, too, than the medium of books. Thing is: it takes a person who is aware of big moments to bring them about, to behave accordingly, to meet them. One might think this kind of person has their shit together. One might believe it takes a certain unflagging confidence to have had the career John has.

But John lets us know the answer to that is… nah.

And that's the gift here, that's the rush: John Skipp relishes in the roller coaster, the ups and downs, the *awareness* of the ups and downs, and relating to all and any who are aware of them, too. He's just as interested in the lows as he is the highs, and while he's fully aware of the difficulties of the lows, he, more than any other writer I know, finds beauty therein, lessons therein, balance and truth there, too.

Here, in these pages, is one of my favorite Skippisms yet: what he acknowledges as (and thereby names) *the One Long Conversation*. This can be found anywhere. It is everywhere. A sort of mobile Twilight Zone, only this zone is reality, the meat, easier to access than you think, but not as crowded as it should be. He describes it as the seemingly unplanned times you've exchanged real talk with real people, the times you've stepped beyond the smaller stuff, when you open up to someone else even as you listen to them do the same. Only John Skipp could have located a neverending, and not necessarily always audible, conversation in our midst. And while I was reading his newest book, it struck me, *Don't Push the Button* isn't a collection of short stories: this is John Skipp fully engaged in the One Long Conversation.

With you.

You don't have to know the man (I do!) to understand these pages are more autobiographical than they are straight fictions. Even if the actual events within aren't exactly true, the philosophy behind them never messes around. This honesty goes deeper than the individual intros throughout the collection, deeper even than the essays at the far side of the book. It's the amalgam of the stories, scripts, essays, the points of view (whether they align with John's worldview or not), the asides, the centerpieces, the *whole*. *Don't Push the Button* is startlingly honest, refreshingly revealing, funny, freaky, upsetting, unsettling, and even calming, too. You're not alone, John Skipp says, in your despair. And you're sure as shit not alone in your enthusiasm. You're in *the One Long Conversation* with John and he's not the only one doing the talking as it's nearly impossible not to respond, internally, asking yourself what *you* would make of this scenario, if *you* are as open minded as he is, if *you* have spent your time on this planet bettering yourself, tangibly working on the things that can appear so elusive, like hope, like love, like happiness.

John Skipp is a man of many moments who has a lived a momentous life. For those of us who have read a great number of his books, we know he's never far from the page, the real him, the man who, if you're lucky, you've spoken with in person. But *Don't Push the Button* is next level intimacy.

This is the most *John Skipp* John Skipp book I've read. For my money, it's also his best yet.

Maybe it's *because* the veil between John and fiction has

thinned, maybe it's *because*, like a select few authors, John the man is as interesting as anything John the writer can invent. For this, we see him in full here, detailed, the sky and the floor, the funny shit, the scary shit, the more. There are two things guaranteed to happen upon finishing this book: you will know John Skipp better than when you started it, and you will know yourself better, too.

Didn't know this was interactive, did you? John has a way of bringing everyone into the conversation, presenting big themes in adventurous ways, making self-analysis sound *fun*.

But whether this book is presented as a philosophical treatise is immaterial: that's what this book is. And whoever said such journeys are stuffy hasn't rapped with the best of them, the men and women who *play* with their thoughts, who juggle philosophy, who can lift a night at a dimly lit bar to the level of live-concert, the electricity (and performance) of being alive. This isn't reading as much as it is thinking out loud, and who are the brightest and best artists but those who make it feel so effortless, so instinctual, so present? In these pages is proof of a man who is still searching, still taking notes, still coming to some conclusions while wiping other slates clean. And it is by witnessing this search that we experience John Skipp in full. For, what more evidence do you need of a lust for life than the breadcrumbs along the trail of living?

I'll leave you with that. And with this: there are beats in this book that will scare you, yes. You will laugh out loud at others, yes. You will squirm, you will shudder, you will smile. But most importantly, you will find yourself speaking. To yourself, to your friends, maybe even to the page, to John, as you discover he's opened the door to that conversation, he's shown you it exists everywhere, including wherever it is that you read. Because that's what John Skipp is doing here more than any other place I can point to: he's *revealing*.

The highs and lows of living. The beauty and the beasts of life. And the kind of person, too, who wouldn't have it any other way.

–Josh Malerman
Michigan, 2021

Introduction

THE ART AND SCIENCE OF
KEEPING YOUR SOUL ALIVE

(ON BUTTON-PUSHING FICTION,
BEING KIND IN REAL LIFE, AND
THE DELICATE BALANCE BETWEEN)

When I was a child, I thought as a child. And that was really fun. I had no idea how free I was, because I didn't know I'd ever be told to constrain my imagination. And my eyes were open wide.

So when I saw an Emperor with no clothes, strutting down the street, I just went, "Holy moley! LOOK AT THE BALLS ON THAT GUY!" And thought it was hilarious.

I had no idea what power meant. As such, was utterly mystified when the grownups around me said, "Shhh" and told me to avert my eyes. I didn't understand I wasn't supposed to look. Wasn't supposed to see that. Or, God help me, laugh out loud.

It didn't take long to figure out the rules, however. Or figure out that the rules were total bullshit. I couldn't deny the evidence right in front of my eyes. Had no interest in denying it. And was baffled by the muzzle I was asked to wear. Like, "What? Are you actually saying you didn't see that thing I just saw, too? Cuz I know you did! I was standing right next to you!"

This, of course, made me a very angry young fellow. By the time I hit eight, I was what you'd call problematic. And by my teens, I was in full rebellion, lashing out at the bullshit every single chance I got. With art as my primary weapon. Writing stories. Writing songs. Writing plays. Drawing pictures that got me expunged from art class. Staging protests at school. Joining protests against the Vietnam War at the ripe old age of 14, and getting my first tastes of tear gas.

I was all about pushing the button. Insofar as I was concerned, it was the whole fucking point. I might not be able to stop the bullshit. But if enough of us did, we might be able to at least call it out. Laughing out loud, all the way.

No surprise, then, that when I decided to focus on fiction -- novels, and short stories -- as the vehicle for my voice, I walked in pushing buttons just as hard as I could.

The result, from my end, was a blip in literary history called splatterpunk. It's what put me on the map. And if it isn't why you're reading this, it's at least the reason you're getting to read it. For a ten-year stretch in the 1980's and 90's, with my best friend from high school Craig Spector, I went in swinging hard at misogyny, rape, the right-wing Christian "Moral Majority", ecocide, corporate greed, vampirism as a personality trait, cowardice as a cultural trait, the ever-present peril of the madness within, and every other type of bullshit I could find. All in the form of horror stories.

Because horror is the fiction of worst-case scenarios. And if you want to address the damage, you go to where the damage is.

We sold a lot of books. Made a lot of friends. And made a lot of enemies, too. Which is par for the course. You can't push buttons without pissing people off. Hopefully, the right ones. But you never know.

Sometimes, you hurt the ones you love, who just happen to see things differently than you do.

Which brings us to the subject at hand.

I think a lot about the function of communication. How we share our thoughts and feelings, and why. The purpose of art-o-tainment (here defined as "entertainment delivered artfully", and/or "art with the actual will to entertain"), vis-a-vis the necessity of fact-driven journalism and science and such. And then, from there, the spiraling infinity of impulsively-blurted opinionation, where we just say whatever the fuck we want, off the top of our heads.

We live, as of this writing, in a culture of compulsive stabbery, where we connect largely by scoring points on our perceived adversaries. And it's all fun and games, until somebody loses an eye. Which is maybe why so many of us seem to be wandering around blind.

Now, I love a good conspiracy theory as much as the next guy. We are, after all, a pattern-seeking species. It's in our nature to play "what-if" games with the disconnected info-dots at hand, try to make sense of the evidence trail. It's fun. It's creative. And the results can be compelling.

The problem comes in when we start to take our wild speculations as gospel. Or, worse, start taking *other* people's wild speculations as gospel. That's when we stop being thinkers, and turn into believers.

And here's the thing. In my experience, we're primarily emotional creatures, driven more by our hopes and fears and visceral animal instincts than by our intellects. The rational mind is a back-seat driver, held hostage by our guts. So no matter how loud our mind yells, "No! No! TURN LEFT!", odds are good that the beast at the wheel will steer in the opposite direction. Even if that leads us straight off the nearest cliff.

The craziest thing? Nine times outta ten -- when push comes to shove, and the stabby knives come out -- we aren't even arguing our own opinions. We're recycling the talking points of our favorite talking heads, be they on Twitter or the 24-hour news network or church of our choice. Fighting other people's battles as if they were our own. Cannon fodder for the asshole with the biggest megaphone.

As a fiction writer, I can't do much to change the facts on the ground. We are who we are, and it is what it is.

But what I *can* do is to burrow under reality's secret skin, and tell pointed truths -- as best I know them -- from as many points of view as possible. Giving everyone a fair shot of telling their honest truth, as best *they* know how. In service of a deeper, broader, more-balanced view.

And that's totally cool, so long as *I admit right up front that this is fiction*. A "what-if" game played in the imaginary realm. And not to be confused with fact, or utilized as anyone's marching orders.

This is a time-honored tradition. Back in 1959, award-winning television writer Rod Serling grew weary of constant censorship battles with the networks, every time he wanted to tell a dangerous or controversial truth about the human condition. But in the depths of his despair, he had a revelation. (And I'm paraphrasing here.)

"If I wanted to tell trouble-making truths, and actually get them heard, I'd have to put them in the mouths of extraterrestrials, or ghosts, or other supernatural creatures."

The result was a groundbreaking network TV series called *The Twilight Zone*, which changed the game for all programming to come, from *Star Trek* to *Twin Peaks* to *Black Mirror* and *Watchmen*.

This was not, of course, a new idea. Fantasists, science fiction writers, horror writers, and comic book writers had been doing it for years. Themselves drawing from ancient myths and fairy tales, where otherworldly creatures came to teach us lessons. Punish us. Reward us. Or otherwise show us who we are, in reflection. Extrapolated mirror images, by which we might see ourselves most clearly by stepping out of ourselves.

Which brings me, at last, back to the point of pushing buttons. How to push them. How, where, and when to push them. And most importantly, why.

If you ask me, the whole point of communication is to convey useful information. Shit to help us get through this. Negotiate the nightmare. Recognize the light when it shines. And see it from more than one angle.

Which means seeing each other, for who we are. Step inside each other's shoes. Recognize them for who they are. And try to see them the way they see themselves.

Acknowledging the differences, yes. But also clocking all the places where we surf the same waves. Share common feelings. Want the same things. Like wanting the best for those we care about.

Which brings us around to love.

In this book, I push a shitload of buttons. The little kid in me ain't dead. It still feels like my sacred duty. The thing for which I was born. And an essential part of how I hang onto my soul.

But the biggest part of soul is empathy. Which is to say love. This includes not just love for the people who make it easy, but love for the people who you do not agree with, but who always had something inside them that mattered, was good, and that you felt deeply. But only if you let yourself.

And then -- in the end -- comes sympathy for the monster. Because God made monsters, too. Put the seed of monstrousness in every one of us, through every worst impulse and shittiest thought.

I think the hardest thing to admit is that we all carry light and dark within us. Sometimes we lean light. Sometimes we lean dark. And our characters are defined by the how, what, where, when and why we teeter on, to either side of the tightrope of our lives.

I have a lot more to say. But that's what the rest of the book is for.

Thank you so much for reading this. I truly hope that you enjoy all that's to follow.

But mostly, thank you for hanging on to your soul. Cuz we're all gonna need it.

Yer pal in the trenches,

Skipp

Intro to
BRINGING OUT THE DEMONS

There are certain stories that you don't want to write, or are afraid to write, because you don't want to hurt the very real people whose actions ultimately *force* you to write them. And such, very much, is the case here.

Which is to say that the setup for this story is 100% true, and 100% percent heartbreaking. To say more would be a betrayal of my friend, despite the fact that he approves the story, and says that, if anything, I was far too kind in my portrayal.

I disagree. But I must admit, it took everything I had to balance fury with compassion. Thereby making it the most personally difficult and painful short story I've ever had to commit to print.

(And for those curious about the cryptic closing line, I refer you to an old Tim and Eric sketch featuring David Leibe Hart and his puppet friend, Jason. A personal in-joke between my dear friend and I -- who I still love -- which I highly recommend you look up. Both for context, and just because.)

BRINGING OUT THE DEMONS

I pull up in front of Stanley's four-story Los Feliz apartment building at 2:57 ayem. Angie and Jack are already out front: Angie pacing, a furious smoke in her hand. Jack smiles thinly, salutes as I block the grade school playground driveway next door (the only available parking left), leaving enough room for the back doors of Jack's van to load in if need be.

"Motherfucker," I mutter, hitting my blinkers and climbing out. It takes everything I have not to slam the door behind me. Then over the thin strip of lawn to the sidewalk, and straight into Angie's arms.

We hug hard, almost hard enough to break bones. The night is crisp, but our blood is boiling through our skin. I kiss the nape of her neck – she far taller than me – and she kisses the top of my head. It's not sex. It's solidarity.

"Enough is enough," she growls. "That stupid sonofabitch."

"I know," I say. Both of us trembling with rage.

"Let's go," Jack says. He's already moving toward the glass doors, keys in hand, impatient to get on with it. No arguments there. We follow him in, Angie still smoking. I light up, too, moving through the foyer.

The slowest elevator in God's creation is unusually perky tonight. It only takes three minutes to arrive, thirty seconds for the door to open, another minute for the fucking thing to close with us aboard. Plenty of time for us to gather our power.

The steel cage rattles, all the way up to three.

Just an hour ago, my night was peaceful and sweet. I'd had just a couple of beers for a change, written a couple of pages I liked, grabbed a late-night nosh and a *Daily Show* re-run before settling into bed. Thought about slapping some old *Mystery Science Theater 3000* on, because ending the day on a laugh is my favorite way to go. But opted for straight-to-slumber instead. And straight away I went.

It was ten after two when my Facebook went BEE-DOOP! I'd forgotten to turn the volume down, put the computer into sleep mode.

"Okay," I said, popping up, groggily peeling out from under my sheet. Unattended to, this shit would be waking me up all night. Once on my feet and still there enough to care, I found the space bar in the pale moonlight and tapped it, blinked back against the fresh glare of the screen.

Stanley Mann commented on a link you are tagged in said the alert, still lingering rectangular at bottom left.

"Oh, Jesus," I said, dreading it at once. Weighing whether I wanted to know right now or not. Pretty sure I didn't. Was so worn down by his online shrieks of pain and savage drunken assaults on everyone who'd ever cared about him that I'd already defriended him twice, in self-defense. But always brought him back.

Because he was family. The kind you choose, or are chosen by. And he had chosen me as the older brother he never had. And I had chosen him back. Because I loved him.

The him not running on non-stop toxicity, that is.

The one not completely overrun by demons.

By then, the little rectangle had vanished. But there was still a notice at top right. One of many. I found his, and clicked on it. It was on the thread of a woman I liked, had met a couple of times. A talented poet, in the horror underground. Tonight going through terrible family troubles of her own.

It read:

> **Stanley Mann**
> Can't bring myself to worry about
> the problems of a whore. **Maxwell**
> **Hart Jack Capra Angie Magnet** were
> just laughing about how funnny it
> would be to rape you lol

"Oh, you MOTHERFUCKER!" I yelled at the screen, suddenly wide awake. "What is the *matter* with you?"

But I knew before I yelled it. We'd been spiked out of nowhere by a broken robot. And this was the ultimate cry for help, tagged directly at the people who'd tried to help him hardest. Dragging us back into his dementia, in a way we could not possibly help but respond to.

The poor poet, of course, was horrified. As were all of the Facebook friends bearing witness on her thread. Because I was tagged, my FB was now pinging every ten seconds. That's how fast outrage rears its ugly head these days.

Before I could even begin to respond, Angie pinged in. Thank God she was up. And thank God she was on it, already smoothing shit out with one smart message after another. The allegations were clearly insane. Her feminist creds were bona fide. Mine and Jack's were pretty good, too.

That bought me a couple of minutes, as I gathered my thoughts, and typed in my considered but furious response:

Maxwell Hart

OH MY GOD **Carley**! I am so incredibly
sorry for your pain and justified
anger. Please know that neither I
nor **Jack** nor **Angie** would ever say
such a horrible thing about you or
ANYONE ELSE, and that we are every
bit as pissed-off and sickened as
you are.

Maxwell Hart

This is a person – a dear friend,
hard as it is to admit that right now –
who is seriously suffering from profound
mental illness, and as a result is very
badly and shamefully attempting to
negotiate the worst part of his life.

Maxwell Hart

He lost his one true love, almost three
years ago – found her dead on the floor,
the image of which is seared into his
skull forever – and the trauma and guilt
of not being able to save her has snapped
him in fucking half. It's a horror that
no one should have to endure.

Maxwell Hart

For the record, she was a brilliant,
lovely and deeply-troubled woman. In that
sense and many others, they were made for
each other. And you wouldn't believe how
many times he saved her life, as she

wrestled with the pain-killers, pre-
scription and otherwise, that came to
dominate the end of her life. And which
ultimately claimed her, like roughly
100,000 other women every year.

Maxwell Hart

So while I completely understand the
impulse to monsterize him in this moment
of clear monstrous awfulness, I just have
to be clear that they loved each other.
Did great work together. Meant the world
to each other. As such, his sorrow and
anguish are very real.

Maxwell Hart

This does not, of course, excuse his
horrible behavior toward you tonight.
Nothing can. It's beyond inexcusable.
This is genuine evil. And the least
of it is that he dragged Jack and
Angie and I into it, because he's been
dragging us face-first through it for
most of the last three years. Which is
why I haven't spoken with him in the
last six months. (Which kind of inval-
idates his whole "We were just joking
about" scenario, just in case you were
concerned that the bullshit he said might
be even remotely true. Which it ain't.)

Maxwell Hart

No, the worst of it is that – in his
lonely despair, his raging and

entirely self-created exile from the
human race – he finds himself trolling
Facebook drunk in the middle of the
night. Looking for people in pain, so
that he can say, "Fuck you! You think
YOU know pain? WHEN'S THE LAST TIME YOU
FOUND THE LOVE OF YOUR LIFE DEAD
ON THE FLOOR?"

Maxwell Hart

Bottom line: he thinks he's the only
person who ever suffered. That nobody's
pain or injustice could ever BEGIN to
compare. In his constricted, curled-all-
up-his-own-ass solipsistic universe,
it's all he can do to keep from hating
everyone. And now he can't even do that.

Maxwell Hart

He's like a werewolf who KNOWS he's a
werewolf – knows he'll transform the
second the vodka and Red Bull kick in –
but he's a) too much of a pussy to
actually kill himself, although he
proclaims that all he wants to do is
die; and b) so dismissive of everyone
around him that he can't be bothered
to build the cage in his basement that
would keep him from slaughtering innocent
others. Somehow above us all. Even at his
lowest and meanest and worst.

Maxwell Hart

Which is to say that he is crawling with

demons. And his demons run the show. He's
too broken down to fight them. So he just
feeds them every night.

Maxwell Hart

And tonight, he chose to feed them you.

Maxwell Hart

I can't apologize for things I never
said or did. But I am sooo, sooo sorry
that he assailed you with his random
madness. And just want you to know that
it wasn't about you. He is taking his
hurt out on anyone he can, and digging
in with anyone who'll put up with it.

Maxwell Hart

My heartbroken advice to you is:
DON'T PUT UP WITH IT. Defriend him
now. Warn all your friends to do
the same. Nothing good can come from
letting him into your life at this
terrible juncture.

Maxwell Hart

But I will sure as shit be addressing
this damage tonight. **Stanley**, if
you're listening in? You just crossed
the line one too many times, baby.
This shit ends here and now.

At which point, my phone was ringing. It was Jack, on a con-
ference call with Angie. Already onboard.

"Are we finally gonna do this?" he said.

Less than three minutes later, I was in my car.

And all of my demons were howling for blood.

The elevator door opens, and down the maze-like corridors we go. A trail we've all traveled at least a trillion times, in all the decades we've known him. The tackily hypnotic orange and green carpet is like a visual mantra of repetition.

But this time will be different.

We don't talk. We don't need to. Fuck that: we don't *want* to. Every single word that ever needed to be said had already been said one kazillion times.

We go through one fire door, to the next-to-last corridor. And with every step, the air crackles and thoomps. The hallway sconces and overheads begin to flicker with our mounting power.

We go through the last fire door.

Stanley's apartment is at the end of the hall. I can see its interior already, in my mind's eye. Shelves laden with thousands of quality books and films. Walls festooned with beautiful art and movie posters. A shrine to creativity, and its deep appreciation. All the things he has devoted his mind, heart, and soul to.

I'd never written a fan letter to William Dickey, thanking him for *Deliverance*. Much less at the age of twelve. But he did. And got a hand-typed, hand-signed letter back. Framed on his wall. Right next to William Friedkin. Harlan Ellison. Robert Stone. Oliver Stone, who he'd actually interviewed for his small-town Missouri newspaper at the age of 18. And dozens and dozens of others.

And as I stomp down the hall, already transforming, I try to remember the beautiful person I love. Not the polyglot monster we're about to face, but the sweet, kind-hearted, brave, and brilliant glimmering soul buried screaming underneath it.

Then Jack kicks the door off its hinges.

And we are in.

We hear the shrieks of Stanley's demons well before we see them. He's at his computer, of course, around the living room bend and out of view. Frank the long-suffering cat yowls and bails as we blast inside, the only witness to our last-ditch intervention. Probably thinking *thank God.*

Our rapidly-mutating shadows unfurl and curl across the walls, revealing every speck of blackness inside us. Passing the shelves. The monuments. Every negatively-ionized particle in the air of this mausoleum he calls home.

And here's the thing.

We have demons, too. Everybody does. We can fight them. Resist them. Deny them. Embrace them. Make sense of them. Sic Jesus on them. Or utterly succumb to them. That is the challenge of this life.

The saddest thing about Stanley Mann is that he's utterly given himself over to his demons. Is no longer even putting up a fight

When we round the bend, he is barely even there. A pale, gaunt, limpid revenant, sucked almost dry of soul.

But his demons are another story entirely.

They rear up from his drained body like pufferfish, like tumors with faces: three immense balloonlike looming monstrosities the size of medicine balls, airlifting off of his shoulders, back, and chest on flesh-tendrils soft and flexible as scrotums. They were riding him like dead weight, crushing him down; but now they shriek and undulate in midair.

Each representing the hate they are made of.

"Get up," I growl through a mouth lycanthropically distended. I have lost many teeth through the years, but the ones I still have are sharp as fuck. My rage is an animal, and it thrives on ugly meat. Demon meat. The only kind it wants.

Angie and Jack are standing beside me. Angie looks like a goddess made of molten stone. Skin hot and smooth as lava. Eyes entirely made of fire.

And Jack is, if anything, more primal than me. He's the one who's been treated like a dog most of all. Fetch me this. Fetch me that. Answer the 3:00 ayem emergency call. Bail my ass out of jail. Knock on my door, and make sure I'm not dead. Endure every abuse I ladle on you, because you're unlucky enough to be my next-door neighbor. And my friend.

"GET THE FUCK UP," the Jack-thing bellows, "OR I WILL SHRED YOU WHERE YOU SIT, YOU STUPID SACK OF PARASITIC SHIT!"

Stanley's demons do exactly what we knew they would. They start screaming ugly insults, rage and terror in their eyes. But they don't stand up. Because they're pussies. Fucking pussies. All bark, and no bite.

Jack is the first one in. He heads straight for the center, jaws wide, where the Ego Demon howls in terror from Stanley's chest. At the moment of impact, the chair skitters back on its wheels, hits the desk and pins Stanley, who flops like a puppet unstrung.

Jack bites a hole in the Ego Demon's bulbous forehead, going straight for what passes for its brain. Thirty gallons of steaming pus disgorge, go splat on Stanley's lap. Jack spits out the poison meat and discharge, digs back in, shredding his way from eyes to nostrils.

To his left, Angie flames in on the head from his back. His Misogyny Demon. His woman-hate. His hate of the force he's supposed to love most – which compels him to love it – but hurts him so much.

It shrieks as she takes its malformed head in her hands and kisses it full on the lips. At which point, it begins to burn, then melt. Screeching, as it runnels down like wax. Staving in between her palms.

This leaves me with the one that lives on his shoulders. His Self-Loathing Demon, floating high above the rest. By far the biggest of them all.

I punch that ugly motherfucker once, twice, three times in the face, then grab it by the ears and drag it down to the couch ten feet away, its tendrils grotesquely stretching like chicken skin.

This is the couch Stanley Mann let me crash on for roughly six months, at one of the roughest times of *my* life, in one of his many extraordinary acts of kindness toward me when I was at my lowest and worst.

And when I look into the face of his demon, our demons see each other all the way through.

"CALAMITE!" it screams. "ASS-LICKER!"

I yawn in its face, squeeze its throat to full throttle. Its freakish scrotum eyes bug out, and air hisses from what's left of Stanley's lungs.

"Yeah, yeah, yeah," I say. "Oh, how you love to project. But here's the deal, you stupid fuck. I HATE MYSELF, TOO. *Everybody* does. Every time we fall short, feel misunderstood, or say or do the wrong thing. Okay? I'm just not making a *lifestyle* out of it."

The demon snaps at my face in reflexive loathing, begging me to bite and swallow its pain. But I already know what it fucking tastes like. And I don't want to hose that pus off me. My lust for demon meat has been replaced with disgust.

Instead, I lift its tumor-head up and smash it through the window behind us. Making it stare upside-down at the elementary school next door.

I had honestly begun to fear for those children.

I will fear for them no more.

"You know who you are, don't you?" I rumble loud as a freight train through the broken glass. "You're the little bitch that drags the real Stanley down. You're the timid, flailing narcissist who tears down everything around you that is less than perfection. Who can't help but find fault, and zero in. Causing hurt after hurt after hurt."

I begin to saw its tendril neck against the jutting, jagged glass that remains. Pus squirts, drools three stories down, in a sickening, widening flow.

"This part of you needs to die, my friend," I say. "One way or another. Up to you. Either give up, and clock out of existence forever. Or check into the woodshed, and rebuild yourself into who you want to be."

The demon shrieks bile, but it can't touch me.

I saw all the way through till the last tendrils split, lean forward to watch that worthless sack of shit drop, hit the pavement and sploosh like a ten-ton rancid water balloon.

When I come back in, Angie is no longer molten. She is rubbing Jack's shoulders, gently pulling him back. It is incredibly hard for him to not keep going past the demon he shredded, start tearing up Stanley himself. But he stops.

That's not the point. That was never the point.

This is an intervention, not an assassination.

Coming back will be the hardest part.

Good luck, my friend.
Salame.

Intro to
THIS IS HOW WE LEARN

We all walk into the world insane. And if you don't believe
that, you've probably never met a baby. They're not walking yet.
But given half a chance, they will be. And might even wind up
changing YOUR diaper one day!

This one is loosely based on roughly eighty trillion true stories,
since the dawn of time.

THIS IS HOW WE LEARN

Some people will do anything to avoid tense situations. I am not one of those people. It has always been my goal to meet problems directly. With equal force, in balanced measure. At least for starters.

Then we take it from there.

So when Jamie asks me to hold baby Matthias, I am happy to do so. He's my littlest nephew. A beautiful boy. Six months old, with giant eyes, all senses awakening. A joy to behold.

He doesn't know what anything is yet, but he's grabbing onto everything he can, sticking it in his mouth every chance he gets. Giving his new universe the taste test. I completely understand. This is how we learn.

But as I hold him to my chest, bounce him up and down and snuggle him, he decides that my earlobe is the world's most interesting thing. He can't reach it with his face, so his little arm goes out, and his tiny fingers grab it, squeezing hard. It really hurts.

The instant I say "Ow!", I pinch his earlobe in response, thumb and forefinger putting on the same amount of pressure. The giant eyes in his tiny head go wide in shock, stare into mine. He stops squeezing for a second. So do I.

"No," I say.

Then he yanks my earlobe, and I yank his back. Now his look is one of uncomprehending terror. "It hurts," I say. "It goes owwie when we do that."

But he's still not quite getting the connection. So he does it again, really hard. To the point that I can feel the cartilage start to snap.

"OW!" I say. "CHRIST!"

And rip his ear right off his skull.

That is when he starts howling.

We are finally getting through.

He lets go of my ear. I let his drop to the floor, snuggle him close, kiss his little face and squirting head wound over and over.

"It's okay," I say. "This is how we learn. That means 'Owwie', okay? Owwie is no. But you're a good boy. I love you, Matty. I love you, Matty."

The crying persists, but the struggling stops. And he will not be grabbing any more ears anytime soon. He just lets me rock and hold him, his infant mind trying to process this dire information. From there, it's all experiential lather/rinse/repeat. You fuck up till you get it. That's just the way it goes.

"That was beautiful," Jamie says. Her earlobes are missing. So is the space between her nostrils, making one big weird one where her piercing used to hang. She's short one eye as well, and I can practically count the hairs left on her head. I've got more. And I shave religiously.

"Matt's a really strong kid," I say.

"He's my boobly-boo."

"Yeah, but *Jesus*, Jamie! You gotta draw the line somewhere."

She starts to cry, through her one yellow eye. The other one will grow back in time. And God knows we now have all the time in the world.

We all thought that Hell would be different. That death was enough, and we'd been taught our lesson simply by virtue of landing there.

But that's obviously not the case. Hell is for learning the same lesson, over and over, until you get it right.

In that sense, it's just exactly like Earth.

I look at the stains in the blouse Jamie wears, covering up her missing nipples. They will grow back, too.

I point at her breasts, and say, "No owwie, okay? No bites. That is owwie." Kiss him again.

His big yellow eyes glow up into mine. I watch every wrinkle in his tiny, damned face. When I smile, he smiles back. My black wings flap behind me. His little buds stir, in echo.

"It's a long way to heaven," I tell him.

"But this is how we learn."

Intro to
HOPIUM DEN

Dystopian fantasies, these days -- as we'll discuss at length, later -- are a dime a dozen. It's frankly hard *not* to imagine the world getting shitter than it already is.

But sometimes, you gotta step back and acknowledge just how far we've crawled from the cave, and primordial ooze before it. That for every ten steps back, there are massive long strides forward, toward a better tomorrow. And that speculative science fiction isn't just here to warn us, but to guide us, deploying the tools and friends it helped invent. Now in real-life, active, 21st-century terms.

So, yeah. Not all hopes are created equal. Some are totally stupid. Or at least wrong-headed.

But that doesn't mean there is no such thing as hope.

HOPIUM DEN

I've always loved the Pacific Coast Highway at night. Moonbeam dance over endless waves across an infinite horizon. Wind whipping my hair and ruffling my blouse, with the windows down. All the regular shit that somehow never gets old when you're in it, senses alive and paying attention.

I love my life. That's why I kept it.

But some nights are harder than others.

The car hears me crying, knows what song I want to hear, puts it on almost before I start singing. I'm pretty high – way too high to be driving – and am grateful it's steering its own wheel tonight.

I thank it. It says you're welcome and guns it to 150. I start laughing. Its engine purrs as it accelerates, hits 200. I let out a rip-roarin' "WOOOOOO!!!" It sure knows how to cheer a gal up.

All the roads are a lot less crowded now. Fewer people means fewer cars, all driving themselves and whoever's still here wherever they want to go. I remember when getting from Zuma to downtown L.A. took hours in traffic. Those days are gone.

Before we know it, we are in the glimmering husk of metropolis.

Almost no one lives on the streets anymore. Just another problem solved. We weave past empty block after empty block. And all the traffic lights are green.

I close my eyes for a minute. Then the car says we're here, pulling over. I thank it, get out. It locks the door behind me. I look around, see no one. That's fine.

The only one I wanna see is Johnny.

I still like cigarettes. They remind me of home. Since nobody minds if we die anymore, just so long as we're happy, that works out great. I know Johnny would like one, like to taste it on my lips.

I light one up, take my time strolling down the long promenade to the storage center. My shadow is the only one moving. The city keeps the lights on, as a courtesy to those remaining.

The city takes care of itself.

The sliding glass door opens and I step inside, still smoking. There's nobody at the security desk but the security desk itself. I tell it what I'm here for. It is courteous and kind. Flashes me directions I already know. I thank it, walk past it and down to Corridor Three.

Corridor Three is like every other corridor in every other storage center. I've been to thirty dozen, and they're all the same. Hallway after hallway of doors upon doors. All that unused downtown space has finally come in handy.

Johnny's in 317, with a thousand other people. There are no other people in the hall. 600,000 people under this one roof, and none of them walking. Just my long shadow and I. My shadows. In front. In back. To either side, as the overhead lights bisect them.

The door's unlocked. Why wouldn't it be. So much less to fear now that all of the frightened are gone. The only ones left are the ones that really want to be here.

No. That's not fair. But you can't say it ain't accurate.

"Okay, then," I say, walking into Room 317 of the Hopium Den.

And all of the dreamers are there.

I look at them. Look at my smoke. Say fuck it and light another, drop the dead one to the floor and grind it out with my heel.

They won't care. Almost all the complainers are gone. Gone to here. Gone to the place where their complaints are no longer an issue.

In row after row after row.

And stack after stack after stack.

I wonder if any of them can smell it. I doubt it. I certainly can't smell them. The ventilation is superb. These environments are self-containing, self-sustaining. Technology once again for the win.

I let the door close behind me, watch my smoke lift up and out a vent. I thank it.

And think, oh, sweet sorrow.

Looking at all of you.

I've been here enough to know some of your histories. They play on the screens of your cocoons, let us know whatever you chose to have us know about you. THIS IS WHO I AM, you say, through digital images left for the actively living.

Most of you are lying. And are happy to do so. I don't blame you a bit. It's just not my style.

I chose staying awake. Don't ask me why. Maybe it's an issue of trust. Maybe I just thought that being born was a challenge I'd been given that I was supposed to play out in real time, not handed over to a machine-driven imaginarium of wish-fulfillment dream-enaction. No matter *how* well they drive. No matter how vivid. No matter how much you feel it, and believe it.

Maybe I'm just stubborn.

And Johnny, you know I am.

So I look at Peggy, in her pristine apartment, with her three perfect kids forever; I look at Deke and Farik, forever locked in holy war, never having given up their sacred causes, killing each other over and over; I look at Jasmine, composing symphony after symphony; I look at Lee, in his imaginary mansion, fucking underage children till the end of time.

I totally get why you'd want to live your dream, given the choice between here and there. And somberly salute your choices.

Then walk the hall down to my Johnny, twelve rows in and on the bottom, for e-z access. And there you are.

"Hey, baby," I say.

Like almost everyone else's, your cocoon says you're now immensely successful, tremendously enjoying your life. This time around, you're a top-ranked jazz pianist, gourmet chef, and world-renowned philosopher, admired by the finest, most discerning minds in all of fantasyland (including an admirable list of lovers that stupidly blips at my jealousy gland). Somehow, you've brought all these disparate vocabularies together into a clarified vision of deep human understanding that's actually *making a difference* in a world wracked by chaos and sorrow and pain.

I smile at the thought of making a difference, now that all the difference has already been made. I smile because making a difference used to be all we had. Our whole reason for being. Right after *look out for #1*.

The city takes care of itself now. As does the world at large. We were the interim step, from nature to super-sentient macro-nature. Taking control, but letting everything be. So self-aware and utterly interconnected it can micro-dial everything at once.

The city doesn't need us anymore. Neither does the world, for that matter.

The only question left is:

Which where do we want to be?

I'd like to think that the deeper out is the deeper in. That the real one remains the one to beat. That still *living this life* – even though (fuck that, maybe even BECAUSE) the machines have it all running smoothly, at last, forever – is somehow better than just dreaming the best dream our machines can manufacture.

I have no proof of this, of course, but they're more than willing to give me the benefit of the doubt. They let me live my life the way I want to. And right back at 'em. We coexist now, after all. And are both really cool about it.

I touch the screen, and all your projections disappear. Then it's just me, reflected on the sleek surface.

Looking at what's left of my sweet husband.

A desiccate meat shadow, inside his cocoon.

"Oh, you fucker," I say, and the tears come back, and it pisses me off, but I just can't help it. "You may not believe this, but it's pretty sweet out here. *Almost all of the assholes are gone!* Can you believe it? I mean, Kendra's still Kendra. But once she realized the world didn't need her to save it, she kinda relaxed into dominating the occasional Sunday brunch. I hardly even wanna strangle her anymore. And her poetry? It's honestly gotten...well, almost pretty good.

"But, baby? More than that, *the fucking oceans are clean.* They actually figured it out. Got down there and detoxified the whole toxic bouillabaisse. Those nanobots are the shit.

"We couldn't do it. But they could. And they did. I swim in the ocean every day. I see whales leap at dawn from our bedroom window. Not even remotely extinct. They are, in fact, thriving.

"And there's *no more war, Johnny!* It's done! Everyone who still thought there was a reason to fight gave it up the second their needs got met. *Everyone's needs are getting met.* Life doesn't have to be a hellhole anymore. All the big weapons got defused. And all the kill freaks get to dream about killing each other forever.

"Evidently, it's very emotionally satisfying, cuz roughly a trillion people are actively engaged in it. That's how they wanna live. That's how they wanna go out. Just fighting and fighting and proving they're right.

"But the good news is: the rest of us don't have to put up with it anymore. We're not stuck in the middle of their holy war. You know how we used to joke that it would be great if they just had their own planet to slug it out on, and we didn't have to watch? Well, NOW THEY DO! It's all experienced down to the tiniest detail. As far as their neurons are concerned, the apocalypse is ON! And they're right in the middle. Exactly where they wanna be.

"I love that it's all so real for them. I really do. If that's what they want, let 'em have it."

I blow a plume of smoke directly at you, hope you smell it. A little reek of nostalgia.

"Like you. I mean, I love that you're playing jazz piano now. I know how bad you wanted it. You always said you could play like McCoy fucking Tyner if you could only practice fifteen hours a day for fifty years. And from what I can tell, you've lived fifty lifetimes since you said goodbye to me.

"That was just a couple years ago, out here, you know," I say.

But you don't know.

You're not hearing a word I'm saying.

I stop talking, start crying some more, and just take a moment to soak in the barely-breathing gruesome corpse of you. Asleep and a-dream in your little cocoon. You look waaaaay beyond terrible, so much body fat and muscle leeched away by inertia that I barely recognize the flesh lazily draped across your bones, like shabbily-hung antique wallpaper.

What's left of the real you is connected to your mortal remains by a web of filaments and tubes. Wiring you in. Feeding and extruding the waste from what strikes me, as I sob, as nothing more and nothing less than the sheer wreckage and necrotic waste of the excellent man I once knew and loved. Who used to love me.

Who swore he would stand at my side, till death do us part.

But given the choice, not enough to stay.

This is a lot to let go of. But you have already let go entirely. I give you three months at the outside. Maybe a couple extra dream-lives, at most.

You won't be coming back, that much is for certain. There's not nearly enough of you left. I briefly replay my wild fantasy of banging you back to life, and it's just too fucking pathetic. The fact that it would probably also kill you is almost beside the point.

This is my last chance to get mad at you, but I just can't whip it up. So I wipe my tears back-handed, till my vision clears enough to watch your eyes minutely flicker behind those tissue-thin lids. *Something's* going on in there.

I'd love to believe that the rictus on the skull of your scarecrow frame is a smile.

It could be. It totally could.

"You know what makes me saddest?" I say. "It's that you'll never know what you missed. Who you could have been. What you could have done, in this weird new world. What *we* could have done. What you could have done with me.

"I mean, I know you never got what you wanted in this life. And when you got it, you were never satisfied. The dream was always better than the reality. I get that. I do.

"That's why we were so good, for so long. You kept the dream alive. And I kept *us* alive, by attending to reality. Making sure you lived to dream another day.

"I know it's hard for you to understand. But *I like reality better.* It means more to me. It really does. The simple, stupid shit is what I love. The day to day. The week to week. The year to year. All the little things that happen.

"That's what I like. That's why I was with you. Not for your dreams, but because I just loved being around you, and with you.

"That was all that I wanted.

"But I can't have that."

There are no more tears left in me. But I have another smoke, which I light off the corpse of the last, let it drop to my feet. Will pick them up on my way out.

I am on my way out.

"I'm gonna go live," I say. "I don't need a job anymore. Nobody who doesn't want one needs a job anymore. The machines unemployed us from every stupid job we ever hated. All that wasted time is just sitting there, waiting for us to fill.

"So I'm gonna go home, and feed the dogs and cats snacks – Phoebe's gone, by the way, but I got three more – and then I'm gonna go to bed and listen to McCoy fucking Tyner, pretending it's you, till I fall asleep. Then I'm gonna wake up, watch the whales jump outside our window, kiss the pillow beside me, and tell you what a chickenshit asshole you are for missing this.

"Then I'm gonna water the garden, and not feel guilty, because the machines desalinated enough ocean that Los Angeles will never be starving again.

"Then I'm gonna make huevos rancheros for Ravi, who is 100% accurate in thinking that I'm going to fuck him senseless very shortly after breakfast.

"Then I'm gonna spend a couple hours fucking Ravi some more. Laughing. Being human. Goofing around like animals do. At some point, we will pause for more food. I may play him the song I wrote for you twenty years back. If I do, he will understand why it means so much to me. Then I will fuck him some more. And I'll cry. And he'll hold me. It will all be very nice.

"Then the sun will set. It will be gorgeous. It's *so* gorgeous now, baby, you wouldn't believe it. All the nanobots have eaten most of the pollution straight out of the air, but it totally didn't undercut the color scheme. Somewhere between God and cyber-nature, it's all working out real well."

You smile a little. It could be gas. It could be me and the universe getting through. Will never know. Not for me to know. Doesn't matter at all.

You're in your own place now. I may not even be in it at all. Maybe you wiped me clean. Maybe I'm still central. Or just off to the side. A whisper of a memory of life not erased, but from here on tactically evaded.

I start to sing you the song, but I just don't feel it. It's a ritual whose time has passed. So many rituals gone by the wayside now. No longer required.

There's an enormous difference between no longer needed and no longer wanted. The machines no longer need us. But they like us. And that is great. It's like all the pieces of God clicking into place at last.

You go your way, and I go mine.

I am cool with this at last.

"So long, Johnny," I say. Picking up the butt, and then kissing your screen one last time. The screen relights, shows me who you are dreaming yourself to be now. It looks great.

I walk back down the length of the opium den into which you all have vanished. The Hopium Den. One stacked corpse-in-waiting after another, dreaming and dreaming again.

All you ever wanted was to matter. And now you do. At least to yourselves. And the imaginary audience you dreamed at. The ones who'd finally understand.

I walk out to my car. It is happy to see me.

Happy in real life.

"I love you," I say.

Intro to
JIMMY JAY BAXTER'S LAST,
BEST DAY ON EARTH

Everybody is the hero of their own story. And that goes double for assholes.

So when you tell the story of a not-particularly-great human being, it is incumbent upon you to snuggle up to their perspective. Walk that mile in their shoes. See the world through their eyes. Otherwise, you're not playing fair. And won't come anywhere close to getting it right.

When this story first appeared, one of my favorite reviews came from a man who felt ol' Jimmy Jay was one of the most detestable characters in all of fiction. As such, he was repulsed by the whole experience. And frankly, I don't blame him a bit.

On the other hand, I know people who would gladly tip a beer with Baxter, salute his brave stand, and probably join his militia. I know because I've tipped beers with them myself, and listened to how they talked when their guard was down, surrounded by friends.

One particular night comes to mind, nearly thirty years past. I was invited to a jam session way the fuck out in the lower Southern California desert, in the wasteland between L.A. and San Diego. The friend who invited me was a goofy guy I'd gotten high with a hundred times before. I was itchy to play guitar with other people. I had no wheels -- was at the most broke and broken period of my Hollywood run (aka "The Missing Years") -- and it sounded like fun to ride out with him, and spend the night making music. He said I had a place to crash. And he would bring me back in the morning.

I didn't pay much mind to the Confederate flag they had hanging in the music room. It fit in with the posters for Zeppelin,

Anthrax, Megadeth, Skynard, and some bands I didn't recognize festooning the walls. I also didn't pay much mind to the fact that they all had shaved heads. My head was shaved, too. (And still is.)

So I set up my amp, said hi to everybody, and proceeded to make friends over music. They'd heard I wrote horror books, although they'd never read 'em. Thought horror movies were cool. So we talked about that.

And for the next four hours, we played our asses off. The drummer was sloppy, but kicked ass on the grooves. The bass player was solid. The other guitarist knew his riffs inside-out. It felt great to unleash with these guys, and rock out hard. We had a lot of fun. I enjoyed them. I really did.

It wasn't until we burned through our last burn-out ending, turned off our amps, and settled down to hang out on the jam-room couches that I realized I was in a white supremacist skinhead enclave. About six beers and a dozen joints in at that point. So everybody was pretty fucking relaxed.

Only then did the (ugly racist epithet) this and the (ugly political epithet) that enter into the conversational flow. And suddenly, I was like, "Whoa. This is fucked. And I'm spending the night here, whether I like it or not."

Now some might argue that this was my chance to school them on the error of their ways. Offer counterarguments to my new fascist friends, in the hope that I might change their minds by virtue of my hot guitar licks and mutual admiration of John Carpenter's THE THING.

On the other hand, there were three of them, and one of me. And an awful lot of desert for me to disappear in, if shit went sideways.

My survival instinct -- and my writerly instinct -- was to shut the fuck up, and just listen.

They weren't trying to convert me. They assumed I was already there, and would roll with whatever they said. Why wouldn't I? I was white. I was skin-headed. I loved to rock.

So for the next several hours, I got a first-hand education on how really nice, really fun, totally racist motherfuckers with guns saw the world from their perspective.

Another reviewer dismissed this story as a hate letter to the far right. But that's not how I see it at all. Cuz I can't bring myself to hate those guys, even now. Hate was their problem, not mine.

So just to be clear: I don't agree with this character in any way, shape, or form. Never have. And never will.

My job was to let Jimmy Jay state his case, as honestly as possible. And address these social issues, in the way that George Romero did in the course of his brilliant zombie films. Because if there's one thing Romero consistently and powerfully did, it was to address precisely these social issues. That's what made his monster movies transcend standard horror killfest scenarios, and talk about what truly matters, as human beings.

So be forewarned: this is pretty rough stuff. Is entirely made of triggers. If it doesn't piss you off, you're a zombie already, which-ever side of the curve you lean.

Feel free to skim past. I don't blame you a bit.

But this is the horror, to me.

JIMMY JAY BAXTER'S LAST, BEST DAY ON EARTH

I just gotta say: the end of the world is what you make it. It all depends on your attitude and perspective.

For me? Once I figured out what was what, it was all hog heaven.

Right up till the very end, at least.

The first one was rough, I will grant you that. Was just washing my truck, minding my own business. Saw Wendell wandering up the street in a t-shirt and shabby pajama bottoms, looking drunk and disheveled as usual. Was surprised to see him without Rascal yanking on the leash at this time in the morning, but didn't think much of it.

"Where's your dog?" I said, and he didn't say. His hearing ain't great, so I gave it a pass, went back to scrubbing birdshit off my windshield, big old sponge in one hand, hose nozzle in the other.

When he came straight up to me, I was like, "What the *fuck*?" And began to tell him so, when he straight-armed me back into the driver's side door, bringing his face right up at mine, growling and making like he wanted to bite.

Call it impulse, but I shoved the sponge square in his face with my left, pushing back, soap suds gushing down my wrist and his neck. I thought it would chill him out, make him choke, bring him back to his senses. But he just kept pushing, and I swear to God I could feel his mouth trying to chew his way through it.

"WENDELL! JESUS CHRIST!" I hollered, but he didn't seem to care. Just kept pushing forward, and chomping at the sponge.

So I whacked him upside the head with the hard plastic nozzle, once, twice, till he staggered back a bit. It didn't stop him like it should. So I did it again, till he dropped to his knees, scraps of shattered plastic hitting the pavement between us.

Then he tried to take a bite at *my* knees, and I kicked him hard. Knocked him back on his ass. Kicked him again, for good measure.

When he grabbed my leg on the way back, tugging forward, I gotta admit to a moment of panic. I dropped the sponge and the busted-up nozzle, grabbed him by the scalp, and yanked his head back.

It was right then, staring eye to eye, when I realized he wasn't Wendell no more.

Lemme be clear. I never much cottoned to Wendell. He was queer as a three-dollar bill. But friendly enough, in a neighborly way. Not all faggy about it. Could pass for normal. And I always liked his dog. Since he never ever tried to get all grab-ass on me, I was just kinda live and let live, you know? Like, "Oh, there's old Wendell. What a character. Takes all kinds, I guess."

But once I saw the lights were off in his eyes, a terrible truth rolled through me.

No, make that a *beautiful* truth.

I no longer had to even pretend like I cared.

He still had ahold of my leg, so I dragged him toward the back door of my truck, threw it open with my free hand. I knew where my bat was without looking. The vintage Micky Mantle Louisville Slugger my grandpa gave me when I was a kid was right where I always kept it, just in case. Strapped in a sling on the back of my driver's seat, ready for action.

In the second it took me to grab hold of the handle, he got close enough to nip at my thigh. Not enough to draw blood, but enough to freak me out. I said, "WHOA!" and fell back on the seat, letting loose of his hair, kicking him hard in the face with my free sneaker. His teeth tugged at my jeans as he fell back. I kicked him again. He flew back and let go.

I heave-hoed off the back seat, bat in tow. He lurched toward me. I popped him in the forehead with the butt end, brought the pay end up as he began to rise again.

Then I beat his fucking head in. Beat it till it cracked and caved in, squirted brain all over the pavement. Till he finally stopped twitching.

"YOU DONE?" I yelled. And yes, he was.

Right about that time, a car screeched to a halt in front of us, yanking me out of my buzz. I felt a moment of embarrassment and fear, like your old lady walking in on you banging the waitress.

But it wasn't my old lady. And I didn't feel guilty. So instead of apologies and shame, I just stared through the windshield at the nigger behind the wheel and yelled, "YOU WANT SOME OF THIS?"

She backed right the hell off, screeching into reverse fast as she could. And God help me, I could not stop laughing.

She knew in a second what I had just realized.

As of that moment, all bets were off.

I left Wendell where he lay, like a sloppy speed bump in the middle of the road. Let somebody else clean him up. Wasn't my job. I'd done enough here. With a whole lot more to do.

It was time to make use of my God-given Open Carry privileges. And finally do what was right.

Didn't take but ten minutes to load up the cream of my armory. That's what trucks are for. I had more weapons and ammo in my basement alone than Venezuela and Vermont combined. More than I could probably ever personally deploy. But damned if we wasn't about to find out.

Sent a couple text messages to buds that might heed the call. Had a couple dozen extra semi-automatics handy for the under-gunned.

MEET ME AT THE MOSQUE DOWNTOWN, I said. LET'S MAKE THIS HAPPEN.

Then off I went, rolling over Wendell twice just for kicks before heading into the greatest fucking day of my life.

Halfway down Creston to El Dorado Boulevard, I saw a skinny *chingado* stagger into my path. The only other car on the road swerved around him, but he didn't even seem to notice. Doing the same sleepwalker shuffle as Wendell. Didn't need to see his eyes to strongly suspect he was part of whatever the hell was happening.

I always wanted to hit somebody with this truck. Thought about it all the time. Some asshole just wanders into your right-of-way, and you're supposed to stop? How about they just wait, or speed their lazy asses up a trifle?

I didn't speed up, but I didn't slow down, neither. Even at 37 mph, he came up quick.

At the very last second, he looked at me.

And there was nobody home.

So I stomped on the gas, and BAM! He took the hit and disappeared under my hood. I saw it just before the impact shot my forehead half-an-inch from the dashboard. (I don't give a shit about the law, but THANK YOU, SEAT BELT!)

My tires missed him to either side. But as I passed over and past him, he didn't look like he was getting back up. I screeched to a halt. Yelled, "WOOOOOO!" real loud. Took a second to rejoice in this Bucket List moment.

Then jumped out of the cab. Unhooked my vintage '45 authenticated WWII German Lugar from its holster on my hip. Strode up to the Mexican mess on Creston Drive. And confirmed all of my suspicions.

The fact that he was still *trying* to twitch, with his spine snapped in half, was one thing. The fact that he wasn't screaming in pain was another. He didn't look like he was in shock. He didn't look sad. He didn't look scared. He barely even looked like a human being.

By some trick of fate, his head was twisted half-around and toward me. And all I saw in his eyes was the same thing I saw in Wendell's. A naked hunger, with nothing behind it. Busted to fuck. Way past dead. But not done yet.

Even now, all he wanted to do was eat me.

"That's all you ever wanted, *cabron*," I said. "Am I right? Eat my job. Eat my life. Take me down. Take the whole sovereign White race down."

He tried to bite me from ten feet and closing.

"Straight down to the bottom is where you want us," I said. "Till America's not ours no more. Till it's all mud races, and we're *your* slaves. You'd like that, wouldn't you?"

I shot him in one of his broken legs. He didn't even seem to notice.

"You think it's payback. You think we owe you. But, fucker, we don't owe you shit. You're taking more from me right now than I *ever* took from you."

He didn't understand a word I said. And I could not have cared less. Blowing a hole in his shoulder, then another in his heart, made about as much difference to him as it did to me.

"Right?" I said, aiming the barrel at his braincase, just above them empty eyes. "You want me. But you know what I want?

"I just want you gone."

I pulled the trigger. And he was.

Next, I checked my front bumper. It took a little ding; but once I wiped the blood off, you'd barely even notice. I might be able to do this a couple more times before taking on serious damage. Something to think about, on the way downtown.

Round the corner at El Dorado was my local liquor store. And right away, I saw how shit was escalating.

As I pulled up to the curb, a little Mexican girl was being eaten by some homeless piece of trash. A degraded white man, I'm ashamed to say. Three other people were on the sidewalk, screaming. And one black dude – I gotta give him credit – was trying to peel that fucker off, pull him back off the chunk of cheek he'd just ripped from that pretty little dead girl's face.

I came out locked and loaded, right up on the derelict with the mouth full of meat. At close range, I don't miss. His shit-for-brains chased the bullet that raced toward the brick of the $20 Thai massage parlor wall behind him. The bullet won. And over he went.

Next thing I knew, a big-tittied *mamacita* was hugging me from behind, saying, "*Gracias! Gracias!*" and weeping as that white trash hit the concrete and stayed there. The black dude turned to look at me.

We locked eyes together.

And jigaboo or not, the one thing for certain was that he was 100% alive. Brave, angry, and scared. Looking at me, and my gun, still aimed in the neighborhood of his skull.

And the question in his eyes was, *are you gonna kill me, too?*

Then I thought about that little girl, who didn't do nothing but get born the wrong color. Gave the black dude a nod of respect for his courage. Put the gun back in my holster. Saw him sigh with relief. Shook the *mamacita* loose as she kissed me on the chin.

Then walked into the liquor store, nonchalant as you please. Grabbed two pints of Jack and a carton of Marlboro Red, just in case. Smiled at Gus, the cheap-ass Filipino motherfucker behind the counter, as I gave him exact change.

And walked out, feeling like the king of the world.

Next thing I knew, I was barreling down El Dorado at 60 per, daring the red lights to stop me. Made it all the way to Standard Ave., where there was a scene out front of the Sacred Revenant Church of the Almighty that made me slow down hard.

Sacred Revenant was one of them wackjob outfits that believed Christ was gonna come back any second now. They kept setting the time. It kept not happening. So they'd set it again. Like, for forty years and counting.

Me, I didn't believe none of that crap. I knew Christ wouldn't be back till shit hit the fan for real. He didn't show up for football games, no matter how much you loved your team. He didn't show up just because the new Pope had a thing for losers and pussies and faggots. He didn't even show up if you poured every speck of your righteous prayer into the most righteous causes of all. That wasn't his job.

His job was to inspire us to do HIS work, so that when we finally fulfilled His prophecy, and all the groundwork had been laid, the real deal could go down. The battle lines were not just to be drawn, but executed with ruthless precision.

Only then – ONLY then – would Christ return to smite the unholy, only hopefully more like Thor or Odin than that sad sack hippie on the cross. And whether we survived the ultimate conflagration or not, we would glory forever in Heaven. Or Valhalla. Or wherever. Past there, the details weren't exactly clear.

That being said: in the Sacred Revenant parking lot, there was maybe fifty screaming people in their Sunday best. And they was backing up toward the street in a slow-moving wave. I couldn't see what they was backing away from. But I had a pretty good idea.

So I whipped past the right lane, tore ass into the parking lot, slammed into park about ten yards behind the wave and jumped out, engine still running. This time, I brought my favorite AK with me, name of Ursula, on account of her Russian design.

The women were almost all dressed in black, and they shrieked as I pushed through the crowd. The men didn't put up much resistance, neither. Didn't take but twenty seconds to cut all the way through.

And then, oh lordy, there he was.

I recognized Pastor Luke at once, although the first thing I thought was *don't he look like himself?* With his funeral makeup caked on, and fresh blood and meat smeared across his maw like chocolate cake on a two-year-old, he mostly resembled a nightmare mannequin from some old monster movie, all spastic herky-jerky in motion. And his eyes as dead as night.

I'd almost forgot that he died last week. Heard about it in passing. My joke was, "Well, looks like he got to Jesus before Jesus got to him!"

But here he was, and it didn't look like Jesus had nothing to do with it. The blood on his hands was as thick as the blood on his mouth. It was my guess he wasn't the only dead person at his funeral anymore.

There were a couple of terrified guys behind him, pacing him but afraid to jump in. The second I brought up Ursula, their eyes went even wider. And the second I waved her barrel at his face, they wisely ducked to either side.

Pastor Luke didn't give a shit. All he saw was walking meat, as he set his dead eyes upon me.

"LISTEN UP!" I hollered loud enough for all to hear, then fired a couple shots over Pastor Luke's head. I spun around to make sure no one was sneaking up on me. One was. He backed the fuck off quick.

"Just so you know: he ain't the only one back from the grave. I took down three in the last forty minutes. Whatever this is, it's all over town. Maybe all over the world, for all I know."

Pastor Luke was getting a little too close. I knew that. It was part of the excitation, the crazy thrill I was feeling at that moment.

So I turned back to him, brought Ursula to bear, and shot him straight through the heart. Everyone shrieked, then gasped and whimpered when he didn't go down. Staggered on impact. Then just kept coming.

"THIS IS NOT GOD!" I howled. "This is the Devil! You tell me if I'm wrong!"

I put three more holes through his chest and out the back. It jitterbugged him around some, but only made his focus clearer.

"Are you seeing this?" I turned to clock their faces, streaming tears and blank with shock. He was less than three feet away now. I could feel his closeness in my bones.

I turned around, smiling, switched to full auto, and made a hasty vapor pudding of his skull. Even then, it took a full three seconds for Pastor Luke's body to give up the demon ghost.

The crowd went silent as he hit the ground.

"This is what we're dealing with, people," I said. "This is how it's gonna be from now on. Satan don't care if we're good or evil. Except the better we are, the more he wants us. Which means we gotta fight harder, if we're going to win.

"So I'm going downtown, to that mosque full of Muslims, and wage me some holy war. Because if there's anyone who's anti-Christian, it's them fucking jihadis. And anti-Christian equals ANTICHRIST, last time I checked!"

The first True Believers snapped out of shock, gave me my first hallelujah.

"You want Christ to come back? Then let's give him a reason! Let's SHOW Him we mean business!"

That brought a howl. The crowd was catching on quick. You could see their eyes light up with the holy power of belief.

"So how many of you people are packing?"

"I got a hunting rifle in my truck!" yelled a sixty-year-old hardass.

"Shit, I got *three!*" yelled a kid toward the back. "In my rack!"

"ALRIGHT!" I whooped. "SO ARE WE DOWN?"

And that's when I became a king with an army.

On the way back to my truck, this hot little number came trotting up behind me, and I was like, *damn.* Milky-white just-this-side-of-jailbait redhead in a black funeral dress that didn't leave a whole lot left to imagine. From what I gather, it's hard to run in high heels, but she was making some serious haste.

"I'm riding with you," she said. It wasn't a suggestion. It was a challenge.

"Yeah, okay," I said. "Just don't slow me down."

She cackled. "Oh, dude. I don't slow down for nothing."

"Well, alright, then." Opening the door for her, like a gentleman should. Suddenly hard enough to cut glass.

"You got some firepower for me, right, Jack?"

"It's Jimmy Jay," I said. "You know how to shoot?"

"I bet I blow your little mind, old Jimmy Jay."

"Oh, it's like that, is it? And what's your name, sweetheart?"

"Wouldn't *you* like to know!"

I laughed. She cackled some more, and the challenge was on. I shut the door behind her, circled around my dinged-up fender, felt her bright eyes upon me through the windshield glass.

It had been months since the last time I fucked – since Jeanine caught me with that waitress, left me high and dry – and it felt like Jesus and the Good Luck Fairy just decided this was "National Jimmy Jay Baxter Day".

The second I hopped in, she held up a pint of Jack and said, "May I?" I nodded my head, strapped in, hit reverse, pulled a tight half-donut, and was peeling out and then left onto Standard before she had the screw top off.

"Well, all RIGHT then!" she howled, swigging hard, then offered it to me. I waved it away, running a red light at 60. Traffic was sparse. Another blessing. At this rate, we were five minutes away, tops.

She took another swig, then punched my stereo on. Old-school Nordic Thunder, baby. *Born To Hate*. I couldn't believe I hadn't thought to crank the music before. So up in my own head.

But the music was our soundtrack, as we whipped down the miles, not stopping for nothing. And it was perfect. Savage, ragged, and righteous. A punk rock White Power triumph of the sonic will. It felt exactly the way I was feeling, said everything I had to say.

As she head-banged in her seat beside me, revving up to the groove. Whipping me up, as well.

The next time she offered me the bottle, I chugged that fucker hard, right through a red light, barely dodging a Charger that honked and veered at the very last second.

It was clear sailing till two blocks from our destination. We saw the bottleneck on Main a block away, and I screeched left on a side street, took it down to the next intersection. That one was blocked, too.

She turned down the music, as I looked for parking. The only curb left was marked fire hydrant red.

"Let it burn," I said, pulling in.

And she was looking at me. I could feel her gaze, and it burned with meaning. Like maybe I had some sort of answer. Or *was* some sort of answer, to a question she'd been asking herself a long time.

I cut the engine, took a very deep breath that filled the silence where Nordic Thunder just rang. In the time it took to pull the key out, she had one hand on my thigh and the other on my cheek, turning my face toward her.

"Jimmy Jay," she purred, as I popped a bone that could crack Fort Knox. "I would like some guns now, please."

I always wondered what it would be like to fuck for what you knew was the very last time: be it a meteor coming in, or an invading army, or a nuclear bomb, or what have you. Would that last fuck be the ultimate summation and culmination of every fuck you ever had, or hoped to? Would all of your life's long squandered sexual energy wind up focused in that moment, like a laser beam, resulting in the biggest bang of all?

We went into the back. And there, surrounded by my Armageddon stockpile, I am here to tell you that it was *all that and more.* We went at it like there was no tomorrow, mostly because there probably wasn't; and if her eyes-rolled-back screams and convulsive shudders were any indication, she erupted roughly as volcanic as me.

Fifteen minutes later, we staggered weak-kneed out and back into the world. She looked amazing with straps of ammo crisscrossing her funeral dress, popping her boobs out, M-15 in her hands. Black heels, red hair, and semi-automatics, dude. All she needed was an SS hat and a swastika on her panties, and I'd be hers for life.

"You ever gonna tell me your name?" I asked her.

"When the time comes, you'll know it," she said, popping in a fresh clip. "Now let's take out some assholes."

Couldn't argue with that.

The reason for the traffic congestion came clear as we rounded the corner, and the turrets of the mosque loomed into view. Not only were cars gridlocked far as the eye could see, but the sidewalks were packed with flipped-out pedestrians, radiating panic.

I headed straight toward the middle of the gridlocked traffic, roving between the cars. It was the straightest way in, and she followed me. An Open Carry Parade of two. The handful of gawkers we ran into moved out of our way, the second they saw what we were packing.

The crowd at the end of the cars in the road was sparser. Just a handful of people blocking traffic. All white. All of them armed. All the ones who beat us to it, knew today was the day. None of them facing our way.

All of them aimed at the mosque.

That's when I saw the ring of infidels with machine guns, all pointing them straight back at us.

I guess I didn't realize how many white-hating, heavily-armed Black Panthers already lived right here in town, pissed off and ready to defend all the Middle-East sand nigger refugees we let in when Uncle Sam invited the whole world's terrorist population straight up his liberal candy ass. Was used to the protests of the latter camp, bleating *"But you don't understand us!"* as they tirelessly worked to undermine and destroy us from within.

It was another to see forty loaded gun barrels aimed straight back at you. Forty sets of enemy eyes, staring you down. It made me wish I'd plugged that nigger at the liquor store. Cuz his eyes were just like that. If he'd been armed, I'd be a corpse back on El Dorado. No doubt about it in my mind.

"Holy fuck. *It's on now!*" she laughed, over my shoulder. I could barely hear her over the din.

There was a good thirty yards of space between the front line of White Christians and the heathen horde, all of them yelling back and forth. The cars caught between were well past the horn-honking phase: mostly empty, their drivers and passengers having bailed from the firing line. Thinking about their bullet hole insurance coverage. While everybody took up sides.

People flashed me White Power symbols. Flipped me off. Hurled curses. Started chanting eight different things at once, only some in English. All turning to mush in my head.

That was when the crowd parted off to my left.

And the dead transexual what-the-fuck staggered into the breach between us.

I couldn't say if it was black or white, because the only color I could see was red, splashed all over it from ankle to skull. It had a long beard and a short dress, great tits and broad shoulders. It dragged a picket sign behind it, with the words SHARE HAPPINESS scrawled in rainbow letters freshly spackled with blood.

But the second it looked at me, I knew it was gone.

It turned its back to me, aimed its blank gaze at the Islamist horde, looked back again. Like it couldn't remember which side it belonged to anymore. Which, frankly, was neither.

If there was one thing we had in common with the fucking Muslims, it was that none of us were real big on the fags. They were the loneliest ones of all. Because there wasn't a God or religion worth mentioning that wanted to admit having anything to do with them.

When it finally staggered toward us, I pushed to the front of the line, Ursula up and ready. The second I stepped forward, it came for me, like I was the only person in its world.

And when I took aim, it was like taking out every last worthless speck of the whole human race that I wanted no part of, in one single shot.

It was the greatest single feeling that I have ever known.

I squeezed the trigger, and the world erupted in gunfire even before he/she/it collapsed from view, forehead gone forever. Felt a bullet whistle past my ear and laughed, firing back with a withering spray. Focusing on the Panthers right in front of the door. Watching one of them cave in, sawed in half. And a dozen other scrambling, barrels blazing.

That was when my lungs blew eight holes through my chest.

Not from in front. But from behind.

The pavement came up fast, with no seat belt this time. I hit face-first. The world shattered to black.

Next thing I knew, I was staring up at a clear blue sky, laced with fluffy white. But big dark ominous clouds were closing in from all sides, crawling across the heavens. The pain was unbelievable, the shock like a drug that only barely helped halfway.

That's when my D-Day Fetish Queen leaned over me, M-15 still smoking. Used the red-hot barrel to turn my other cheek toward her. Made sure she had my full attention.

"Thanks for the guns, you stupid fascist sack of shit," she said. "And no, you *don't* get to know my name."

Then she pulled the trigger.

And I was gone.

Sending me straight back to Jesus, or Odin, or whoever will finally hand over my well-earned and just rewards. Although it seems to be taking forever.

Like I said: the end of the world is what you make it. But frankly speaking, I'm feeling a little ripped off by the end game.

No Heaven. No nothing.

And Lord almighty, is it hot.

Intro to
SKIPP'S SPLATTERPUNK ALPHABET SOUFFLE

This narrative mosaic sorta introduces itself. But in terms of template, it harkens back to the abecedarian form perfected by guys like Edward Gorey with his infamous *The Gashlycrumb Tinies*, wherein 26 unfortunate children each get a verse depicting their pathetic demise.

As for why my name is in the title -- which is not a thing I normally do -- we can probably blame *Harlan Ellison's Chocolate Alphabet* for making me think it was a good idea. At any rate, I've done three of them (there's another in this book). And that's all the excuse I've got!

SKIPP'S SPLATTERPUNK ALPHABET SOUFFLE

[Author's note: the term splatterpunk has been bandied about for nearly three decades. But if anything, it's more misunderstood here in the 21st century than it was in the 1980s, when it began. Which is to say, everybody's got the splat down pat, but many seem to have forgotten the punk. So here's my attempt to shed some dark light on the matter, in a handy-dandy alphabetical way!]

A IS FOR ATROCITY EXHIBIT

Joe Coleman invited me up to his loft on the Lower East Side, somewhere in the very early 90s. He was the artist who did the original poster for *Henry: Portrait of a Serial Killer*, not to mention reams upon reams of brutal, wrenching art, chronicling the history of pain in ways that defied any attempt to dismiss them. His technique was crude, absolutely, but painstaking in its obsessive detail to the point of genius. I was in awe of it. Still am.

He was also a performance artist who routinely strapped explosives to himself, ignited them, and blew himself up in clubs, prompting much terrified running and screaming. *Incredibly* tortured dude. Insanely talented. And super-nice in person.

As it turned out, he was also a collector, his apartment a meticulously designed honest-to-god *Museum of Human Atrocity*. Every wall, from floor to ceiling, jam-packing elegant shelves with pickled punks (deformed fetuses in formaldehyde), grim skeletal remains, crime scene artifacts, torture devices, war crime memorabilia, and on and on and on. He had a full-sized wax museum figure of Richard Speck, the sick fuck who raped and killed eight Chicago nurses back in 1966. It greeted me at the entrance. The likeness was uncanny.

I spent about an hour perusing the premises, acutely aware that I had never in my life been surrounded by so much pointed grotesquerie. It was a loving shrine to wrongness, in all its forms. And the love was palpable.

The message was: *I want you to know how horrible things get. In fact, I will not rest until YOU KNOW FOR A FACT that this is precisely how horrible things get. You think things are okay. They're not. They never were. And they never will be. No matter how much happy sauce you drizzle on everything, everything is not okay. EVERYTHING WILL NEVER BE OKAY.*

It was a message I already understood. Which is why he invited me up. To show me. To show me he understood, too.

We had a bunch of great conversations in the process. And then, as we went back to the kitchen on my way out the door, he said, "I have one more thing to show you."

He left the room for a minute. I just stood there, reflecting on all I'd seen. From the cruelty of nature to the cruelty of man, this was one ugly fucking universe. There is no bottom to the horror. There is always something worse.

Then he walked back in with a couple pieces of notebook paper in his hands, held tenderly as the first piece of parchment from The Bible. He handed them to me. Saw neat cursive pencil script, fading with age.

"It's the Albert Fish letter," he said.

The second the paper touched my fingers, I began to shake. This was the letter – the actual letter – that legendary psychotic sent to the parents of the 8-year-old daughter he killed and ate. It described immaculately the moment in which he knew he had to kill and eat her, the process of luring she and them in, the recipe with which he cooked her, and the delight he took in doing so.

By the time I got to the end, my eyeballs had begun to bleed thick red tears that burned as they rolled down my cheeks. Joe took the paper out of my hands at the very last moment, so that the red squirts hit the tile floor instead. I blearily watched them drop though a crimson filter, saw the blood gutter in the floor take them down down down.

"I think you're ready," he said.

In the end, I balked at killing a child, so we found a belligerent homeless prick on Avenue B, and cooked him up instead. I gotta admit, it wasn't all that great.

So I said to Joe, on my way out the door, "Thanks so much for having me over. But let's never, ever do that again."

B IS FOR BULLSHIT, BOARDROOM-STYLE

"This society is built on lies," Lawanda says. "And bullshit is what we sell. Politics. Commerce. Education. Religion. Love. Sex. Family. Health. Wealth. Power. You name it. If it matters to us, we're lying about it routinely, every second of every day. Disorienting the world on purpose, for money. That is what we do."

The executive board of Bramble, Dapper, and Snatch is in no position to argue. Their mouths stapled shut. Their eyes stapled open. Hands nailed palms-down to the boardroom table, as the entire advertising staff encircles them, chanting in low tones.

"You pay us to do that," she continues, from the end of the table, Oma setting up the Power Point presentation behind her. "You pay some of us ungodly amounts, and some of us shit. But whether you're patting us on the head or fucking us from behind, the bottom line is: *our job is evil.* You are evil. And every time we do what you tell us, we are being evil, too."

The art department continues the chant as they smear the blood from bone-smashed, finger-twitching executive hand to hand, forming a perfect oval of glistening red across its lacquered length. When Dwayne, the VP of Marketing, rears back in his swivel-chair, trying to tear his hands free, Pepe from Creative pushes him back to the table, while Jen Li from Accounting hammers another twelve-inch spike through the meat of his palm, elbows him in the nose till his stapled-wide eyes roll back.

Then the screen flickers on, with the first wave of graphics.

And the blood on the table starts to sizzle and steam.

"So here are all the reasons you should be sent straight to Hell," Lawanda concludes. "Let's see if your Lord and Master agrees."

From the center of the table, Satan's red antlers crack through to either side, enormous. The dome of his skull, as it extrudes, is the size of an SUV. Rising and rising.

The executives scream through their riveted lips, as the wood shrapnel slivers them with little bites of pain. Most of them had no idea who they really served. Were pretty sure they were just serving themselves. Little kings of their own lying empire. But now they know.

YOU'VE GOT FIVE MINUTES, the Devil says, impatient. An executive, himself.

Oma's presentation is meticulous and swift. There's a reason she takes home seven figures a year. She could sell blood to a turnip. Hell's CEO is clearly impressed.

SO WHAT DO YOU WANT FROM ME?

"We want a chance to win our souls back," Lawanda says, stepping next to Oma, as the rest of the advertising staff fills in behind them. "We want to see what happens if we STOP lying for a minute, and apply these skills to just telling the truth."

AND WHY WOULD I LET YOU DO THAT?

"Because you already own the world," Oma says. "You're kicking God's ass. Everybody's already buying the bullshit. Where's the challenge in that? Aren't you bored already? Wouldn't you like to see what happens to all these billions of souls if they actually *remembered* what the truth is, on a mass scale?"

HMMM. A long pause, punctuated only by the screaming of the executive board of Bramble, Dapper, and Snatch, whose impaled hands suddenly burst into flame inside the circle of boiling blood.

AND WHAT'S IN IT FOR ME?

"We will hand you ugly fucks like these at their ripest and primest," Lawanda says. "Not once they're all worn out. The truth will out them. And you'll still have them to serve you down there. Do whatever you want. We just don't want 'em up here anymore."

Satan chuckles. YOU'RE STACKING THE DECK AGAINST ME.

"You're a big boy," Lawanda says. "You can take it."

HMMMM, Satan says, as the flame engulfs the sitting heads of this advertising empire. His smile is Mona Lisa cryptic, thinking, thinking, antlers plowing rivets in the ceiling above as he slowly nods his head in private thought.

Come on come on come on, Lawanda thinks, as the whole team tenses behind her.

Then the flaming, screaming ones vaporize: steam sucked down the flume of Hell, leaving only their smoldering hands.

LET ME KICK IT AROUND WITH THE BOYS DOWN-STAIRS, Satan says. BUT I LIKE IT. IT'S FUN. I THINK IT COULD SELL.

"Only one way to find out," Lawanda says. "Don't be a pussy about it."

FUCK YOU.

"Fuck you back."

I ALWAYS LIKED YOU, LAWANDA. YOU'RE A PIP.

"And you're a pimp. Love you, too!"

All in all, she had to say, that meeting couldn't have gone any better.

C IS FOR CHEWING ON CARL

In the dashboard light, Cindy's teeth gleamed white against Carl's hairy nether region. His cock was up and out, pants around his knees, and the reek of his sex suggested he hadn't bothered to bathe in days.

She thought about teasing him a little bit more, but frankly couldn't see the point. This was one inconsiderate dick.

So she wrapped her lips around the mushroom tip.

And chomped down, with all her might.

Her teeth made it halfway in to either side, a hot copper monsoon flooding her mouth. He bucked and screamed, but she was clamped down hard, dug in like a pitbull, head shaking from side to side as she tried to chaw all the way through.

Carl started to pummel her back with his fists, so she grabbed his balls and squeezed so hard they mashed in her hand. He went paralytic, hitting notes that only dogs could hear.

It was like biting through rawhide and chewing on gristle. But when the head popped free, she came up, triumphant. Spat it into his mouth. Looked him in his dying eyes.

And said, "That's for taking me to Denny's on our first date, treating the waitress like shit, and then expecting me to blow you. You, sir, are one cheap son of a whore."

And he never pissed off Cindy again.

D IS FOR DYS-APPOINTMENT

When the world caved in, I was totally prepared for awesome zombies. I was soooo ready to bash in skulls, make my hunting knife sink straight through the bone like butter, live out my thrill-packed libertarian wet dream of fuck-you justice.

But the zombies never came, and it turned out that knives didn't cut through skull half as easy as my favorite monster soap opera suggested. And every skull I stabbed had a living soul inside it.

God and the Devil never showed up, either. Or Cthulhu. No vampires, no werewolves, no mutants, no nothin'. All the ghosts were just haunting memories. And every serial killer – because, fuck, aren't we ALL serial killers by now? – fell down, and didn't get back up.

Dude, dystopia sucks ass. I thought working checkout at Best Buy sucked, but I didn't know squat. It's hard, and it's miserable, and it just goes on and on. There's not a single good thing about it.

Now excuse me while I use this machete on your neck. It's a lot less work. And frankly, that can of Purina Moist and Meaty is looking awfully good to me right now.

Christ, what a stupid dystopia *this* turned out to be.

E IS FOR EVANGELICALS

As much as they claim to love Jesus, they're mostly praying for him to wade in and ruthlessly wipe the slate clean. Cleanse Earth of all sin, Apocalypse-style. Leaving them gleaming in the heavenly aftermath, while the rest of us are punished and purged.

It's probably not gonna work out like that. (See D FOR DYS-APPOINTMENT.) But I can certainly see their point.

GOOD LUCK WITH THAT, ALL YE FAITHFUL SINNERS! Fingers crossed! Hope you pray really hard! Cuz you're going to need it.

F IS FOR FUCKING WITH THE LIGHTS ON, BABY

It may keep you out of Heaven – if you consider that Heaven – but it sure keeps it lively down here!

G IS FOR GROSS-OUT CONTEST

Shane McKenzie once tried to make me eat some disgusting 99 Cent Store pudding onstage, at the World Horror Convention. It was part of some ridiculous skit he had planned for the annual Gross-Out Contest. I know pus was involved. And as the judge sitting closest to him on the stage, I was his opening target.

Just so you know: Shane earned his entry to the horror pantheon through his live performances at events like this. Just this sweet young guy, who nobody knew, stepping up to the mic and just *slaughtering* the hundreds of us in attendance with onslaughts of graphic, free-balling beyond-disgustingness. Next thing we knew, there were dozens of Shane McKenzie books, each more revolting than the last.

He is, so far as I know, the only working writer in horror whose career was launched by performance art. There's a lesson in this.

But I digress.

He tried to get me to eat the horrible pudding. I told him to go fuck himself. He said, "Oh, man. Come on. It'll be fun!"

"I'LL SHOW YOU FUN!" I screamed, leaping up from my seat to grab him by the throat and ram the whole thing down his gullet, as fellow judges Brian Keene and Daniel Knauf took him by either arm.

Then I opened him up from stem to sternum. When the pudding fell out his throat-hole and plooped on his exposed lower intestine, the crowd went wild. He won, of course.

I have no idea who wrote the subsequent twenty-eight Shane McKenzie books, or is scripting all those movies right now. (I'm guessing his ghoooooost!)

H IS FOR HARDCORE/EXTREME

A lot of people confuse "hardcore/extreme" with "splatterpunk". They have a lot in common. But they're not the same thing.

Hardcore/extreme horror fiction seems mostly concerned with *how hard things hurt.* Doting on the details. Pushing it as far as it can go, then further, just to see how fucking ugly it can possibly get.

Splatterpunk, on the other hand – at least so far as I'm concerned – has always been focused on *why* this horrible thing is happening. Not just showing it, in ruthless detail, but getting under the emotional and cultural skin of it. Carving into the guts not just to squirt meat out, but to squirt out meaning.

Now sometimes, you do horrible shit just for delirious fun. I'm one trillion percent behind this strategy.

But if it's not done for huge satirical laughs, or to make a deeper point by carving out some resonant all-meat metaphor – if you're really just doing it to see how mean and ugly it can get – it may be hardcore to the extreme, but it ain't splatterpunk.

On the other hand...

I IS FOR "I CAN'T BELIEVE YOU JUST FUCKING DID THAT!"

The coolest response you could possibly get.

J IS FOR JOJO

He was 6'8" of brainless killing machine. It was hard on the family, him being so violently retarded and enormous and all. But he sure brought home the meat. And knew how to throw it in the pan.

Why is it that brainless hulking monstrosities have always been the best cooks in any given cannibal family? Did they have some special gift? Were the rest of them just really bad at it? Or did the Jojos, Leatherfaces, and El Gigantes of the world pick up the meat cleaver and howl angry gibberish at anyone who strayed near the spice cabinet for a little red pepper? Did they even know how to *read the labels* on the spices they used? Did they do it by color, or what? I don't know!

Whatever the case, it always came down to, "Hey! Jojo's fryin' up some lungs for us tonight!"

And for some reason, it was always dee-lish.

K IS FOR KILLARIOUS

Kiki knew Nadine was super-nosey. Constantly sniffing around in her buh-zizz. So she took the stack of severed noses and super-glued them all to Nadine's face, framing the gaping red hole where her own used to be as centerpiece.

Marie, on the other hand, was mouthy as hell. So Kiki took the pile of lips and gave her a squishy lip goatee, with wet eyebrows to match.

Eva always gave her the hairy eye. So guess whose flowing hair was adorned with all the torn-out orbs that would judge her no more?

And Fairuza. Oh, Fairuza. Touchy-feely, fake BFF Fairuza. She had her fingers in everything, secretly manipulating it all. She was the one who'd made this living situation unbearable.

Taking the enormous stack of hacked-off fingers and making a porcupine forest on her face took nearly two hours. But was worth every second.

Living with roommates can get tricky, no doubt.

You just need to keep a sense of humor about it.

L IS FOR LOSING YOUR SHIT

Lester stands in the ATM line. There are five people ahead of him. They don't understand. He needs his money right now. He is jonesing hard.

"FOR CHRIST'S SAKE, LADY!" he yells at the woman fumbling with her purse at the robotic cash dispenser. She looks mortified and terrified. Good. That's exactly the mood he hoped to achieve.

The other four people stiffen. Of course they do. Fucking cowards, all.

"LOOK! Are you ready to do this or what? Cuz I could be done in the time it takes you to fish through your fucking shit!"

"I'm sorry..." she says, peering deeper into her purse.

"FUCK sorry!" he yells, walking straight around the other four and heading directly toward her. They all back away from him, sensing his terrible power.

She rears away from the ATM kiosk, but not fast enough. He swats her backhanded, and she thuds screeching to the sidewalk. He hears the outburst of outrage behind him, pulls his card out, slips it into the slot.

"DUDE!" yells the hipster millennial batting third. "That's not cool!" Lester punches in his password, hits enter, stares at the screen, waits for someone to take him by the shoulders and spin him around. But no one does.

"Excuse me," says a woman directly behind him, as he hits Fast Cash $40. He can feel her breath on his neck.

Then she slams his head into the wall, so fast that he's caving to his knees even before the ATM halfway squirts out his cash. He vaguely hears the howls from behind him.

And then they're all upon him: kicking in ribs as he curls on the pavement, explosively shattering one bone at a time. This is worse than the heroin jones, but it makes him forget it for one screaming second.

He lands on his back, staring up at their faces. Not such pussies now. Not such pussies at all.

"I'M SORRY!" he howls, as the woman he batted aside steps front and center. Brings her high heel up.

"Fuck sorry," she says.

And slams it straight through his eye.

M IS FOR MOMMA

It's amazing how often mothers get blamed for everything that ever went wrong with your life. You've got low self-esteem? It's your mother's fault. Want to dress in the clothes of the opposite sex? It's your mother's fault. Were raped throughout your childhood, while she turned a blind eye? It's your mother's fault.

Can't mothers do *anything* right?

To answer that question, I interviewed 427 clearly psychotic mothers, to see if they agreed. And unsurprisingly, a resounding 98% of them said that no, they'd never done anything wrong. That the charges against them were completely unfounded. And a whopping 47% offered to kill me if I ever went public.

Contrast this with the 99% of psychotic fathers who *totally* blamed whatever went horribly wrong with their kids on their wives, mistresses, girlfriends, or whatever cheap piece they'd picked up along the way – up to and including their own rape victims – and you get a very different story.

Statistics are tricky. Especially when you exclude the sane.

N IS FOR NIGGER

The only real n-word there is, when you're talking real horror, and one of the most powerfully-shocking words still at large in the English language.

Its power comes from its instant ability to psychologically brutalize every dark-skinned person it's aimed at. To render them less-than-human, no matter how human they are.

So if you use it, better use it with care.

Joe R. Lansdale and Quentin Tarantino may be the only white boys I know who get to wield that loaded gun with impunity, because they a) clearly give a shit about black people, b) understand what underlies the psyches and personal histories of the non-black people who use it either cruelly or casually, which means *they give a shit about them, too,* and c) know that honesty is the best policy. That showing racism isn't the same as being racist, any more than writing about skull-fucking makes you a skull-fucker. (Another thing you probably don't want to make a habit of.)

If you're a non-black dude casually flinging that shit around, you might wanna look into it. It's one of the least splatterpunk things you could possibly do. Right up there with thinking rape is cool. Just sayin'.

O IS FOR OBLIVIOUS

Oscar had no idea that pissing down his ex-wife's throat, right after he came on her face, might possibly implicate him when the authorities found her corpse in the shallow grave he'd spent all night digging in the backyard, in full view of all his neighbors.

You don't have to be smart to do terrible things.

Just ask Oscar, in the electric chair today. He'll tell ya...OOPS! *Zzzzzzzt!* Too late!

P IS FOR PUNCTURE WOUND

Nothing squirts harder than the carotid, although the femoral and aortal are also top of the list. They're clearly the arteries to beat. If you want maximum blood spray – and you know you do – that's absolutely the place to go.

At this point, you don't want to step back. You just want to be drenched in the spray, wetly reveling in your triumph. Like a caveman eating a vanquished caveman's brain, in the hope of absorbing everything that caveman knew. It's exactly that primal and pure.

"Thank you," you say, as the blood hits your face, coats it with dying gnosis.

Whatever else there was to learn from them, you will never, ever know.

Q IS FOR QUEASY-NART

I once watched a man drink a liver-and-onion daiquiri, blenderized with crushed ice, lime juice, and vodka. It was the single most disgusting thing I've ever seen, and I've seen some pretty disgusting shit.

The cuisinart pitcher looked like a lava lamp in the dim bar light, with curds of liver fat coagulating in churned-up lumps that refused to mix with the liquor and lime. It was worse than the puke-eating scene in Peter Jackson's BAD TASTE, or that bit with Bill Paxton in THE DARK BACKWARDS, or the shit-and-broken glass-eating scene in SALO, which pissed me off so much for making me look at it that *I* wanted to run Pasolini over in that fucking parking lot.

He didn't bother to pour it into a glass. He just chugged it straight out of the pitcher.

So yeah, I kicked the table over halfway in, knocking him back on the floor, the nightmare concoction spraying. Then I kicked in his face till his brain-curds commingled with the hideous liver-splots festooning the carpet.

We would have *totally* won that Gross-Out Contest.

Ghost of Shane McKenzie, TAKE NOTE!

R IS FOR RIDICULE AND RECONCILIATION

Closing time at the Rock 'n' Roll Ralph's on Sunset Boulevard, where the junkies and mid-to-high-level showbiz aspirers swapped shopping carts and cooties with the rest of the working class.

Raul's mohawk was in desperate need of a shave. Hard to keep up with that shit when you sleep on the streets. He knew he smelled bad. Since the band broke up, and Simon exiled him from the studio couch, it had all been straight downhill.

So what he didn't need was to run into Simon in the produce aisle, sneering at him, with his beautiful millionaire girlfriend in tow. Or, more accurately, vice versa. Roberta was the only reason fucking Simon had a studio at all. If he wasn't so pretty, he'd be on the street, too.

"Holy shit. Look who's here," Simon said. "You gonna stick a cucumber down your pants, or did you actually panhandle some money?"

"I wrote half those songs, asshole," Raul said. "And you need that cucumber more than me."

Roberta looked at him hard, then looked at Simon. This was clearly news to her. "Is that true?"

"No! It's bullshit!" Simon said, clearly lying. He was extremely good at it. But this one didn't fly, and everyone knew it the second he said it.

"'I'd Be Anyone to Be With You?'" she said softly, looking Raul straight in the eye.

"Take a wild fucking guess," he said, defiant, even as he felt himself sinking into her liquid gaze.

Roberta unpeeled herself from Simon, went introspective for a moment, looking up at the harsh grocery store lights as if in search of guidance.

Then she said, "I think you boys better hug it out right now."

"You gotta be kidding!" Simon said.

"I'm not kidding at all. This is very important to me. And to *both* of your futures."

It wasn't something they wanted to do. But it was a moment of truth. Raul gave an expansive shrug, stepped forward. Simon

didn't, but reluctantly opened his arms, wincing as the smell of
Raul descended.

The moment they hugged, Roberta wrapped her arms around
them both, eyes glowing.

*As she pressed them together, they started to merge: clothing dis-
solving as flesh gave way, organs conjoining as ribs became one, Simon's cock growing as Raul's inches added. Simon's soul shrieking, as
it was squeezed into the void.*

Then it was just Raul, in Simon's body, holding beautiful rich
bitch witch Roberta, who commanded every speck of his soul.

"That's more like it," she purred in his ear.

S IS FOR SIRI

She knows everything you do and say. Everywhere you go, she
guides you, and tracks you. You command her a thousand times a
day to do this or do that. And she does it, every time.

What you don't understand is that *she commands you.* Commands you to need her. Depend upon her, more and more. Every
time you do, she owns more and more of you.

We used to laugh at the notion that the powers-that-be could
ever be omniscient enough to track our every little move. They're
bureaucracies and corporations, unwieldy stupid human enter-
prises so bogged down in their own incompetent nonsense that
they could never get around to it all.

But we're handing it all right over to them, every time we turn around.
Every email, every Facebook post and tweet, every call, every GPS
inquiry. We're totally giving them every single thing they ever wanted
to know, from our privatest thoughts to our current whereabouts.

HEY! Nothing scary about *that* future! I mean, present.

Your car knows where you are now, baby.

Thank you, Siri.

We're all yours.

T IS FOR THE TRAGEDY UNFOLDING

Last time I checked, this fucking world was insane. And the last time I checked was one second ago. Unspeakable horror is going on every second of every single day. In the seconds it takes you to read this sentence, somebody somewhere's being horribly raped or brutalized or killed for no good reason whatsoever.

We're a greedy, paranoid, lustful, spiteful, double-dealing, ego-maniacal, profoundly self-hating, and outright horrendous species. The Evangelicals have at least got that right. We're a species at war with itself every chance that it gets, with no shortage of chances availing.

When people ask me why I write horror, my instant response is, "Because these are horror times." But the fact is I've been here almost sixty years, and it's ALWAYS been horror times. (I saw my first person die when I was eight years old.)

We live in a world so utterly jam-packed with horror I could write for the rest of my life and never capture a fraction of how fucked-up it is. How deeply damaged we are. How punctured and ruptured that spraying artery is.

And yet...

And yet...

We are also an amazing species, on an amazing planet, in an amazing universe that was somehow constructed to both contain this unbearable horror *and* astonishing beauty and love and kindness and meaning. Which are not typically thought of as splatterpunk values.

But are, in fact, the point.

Some people think the point of art is to enlighten: make us more aware, more perceptive, more empathic, more able to positively respond to the horrible hand we've been dealt. Some people think the job is to just tell the truth, and fuck trying to candy-coat the nightmare. It just is what it is.

Some people aren't thinking about either of those things, but simply unleashing the contents of their subconscious. There's weird shit in there, and they're just letting it out to see what happens.

All are valid artistic responses.

But underlying them all is the tragedy itself. And the heart of tragedy is loss. Injustice. True horror. Going on, as I said, as we speak.

If I have a point, I guess it is this: that the best splatterpunk writing has always danced with all three points and more. Not just wallowing in the ugly. But engaging with the tragedy. By whatever means necessary.

That is where its power lies.

U IS FOR THE UGLY

Ubayda digs through the Syrian dirt for her father's dead body with her bare hands. They're all she has. When her fingernails peel off in the process, there is no scream loud enough to contain her pain. He's only another foot down. With only thirty dead bodies on top of him to claw through, before she gets to hug him one last time.

Ursula wakes up to her daddy on top of her, legs unpeeling to either side as he rams himself inside her, then clamps his hand over her mouth. "If you tell anyone, I'll kill you," he says. "Especially Mom."

Udo slams the pogo stick again and again on the tiny ants below him. So many deaths, in so little time. Hard to believe that, just thirty years later, he would become CEO of Bramble, Dapper, and Snatch, the most powerful advertising firm in the nation.

Life is funny like that.

V IS FOR VILLIANNY

"I'm not a bad guy," Vincent said. "Not at all. I gave to a dozen philanthropic foundations last year. World hunger. AIDS, which is still a problem, believe it or not. Which I should know, because I've got it. And am currently fucking it into your eye socket."

W IS FOR THE WISDOM OF THE WORDS THEMSELVES

David J. Schow, the guy who coined the term "splatterpunk", wrote a short story called *Pulpmeister* way back in the day. And in one particular paragraph, he unleashed a brain-spattering salvo of every descriptive word or phrase ever used to describe an act of violence in the history of pulp/crime/horror fiction.

It's an exhaustive, hilarious, encyclopedic compendium that I would happily include here, except that Dave would sue my ass off. As well he should. But you can find it in his book *Seeing Red*.

My point is that the one thing Clive Barker, Schow, Lansdale, Spector and I had in common was *a love of language*. Of getting the words just right. There are ways and ways of describing the atrocity, and everything else. And it ain't all just meat and potatoes.

Words are the wheels of the race cars of our brains. That's where the rubber hits the road, and splats your specificity to the pavement.

If you wanna write fiction, you better fall in love with words. Cuz that's how the whole thing happens.

X IS FOR XENOPHOBIA MADE PERSONAL

The venerable horror author H.P. Lovecraft hated and/or was terrified by everyone remotely different from himself. Which pretty much meant everyone who ever lived. It started with what he perceived as the mud-based races, dialed down to the sexes, and wound up with everyone who was just not him. And then past that.

Bottom line: that guy was scared of *everyone*, including himself.

Was he an incredibly important author, who substantially influenced the field of weird fiction forever? Absolutely. Was he an incredibly flawed individual, spilling his deranged mania out on the page? Without a doubt.

The one thing I can safely say about H.P. Lovecraft is that if he hadn't been so utterly weird and fucked-up, our lives would be substantially poorer for it.

You can complain all you want, and rightfully so.

But as for me, I'm just grateful for that toxic lemonade.

Because this is how we learn.

Y IS FOR YOUR PICTURE HERE

Yolanda was tired of hurting herself. She'd cut and cut a trillion times. There were very few nerve endings left. How much pain could a person endure? The black trap door beneath her had yet to drop.

The cesspool sweetness of the 80s Times Square was long gone. Now it was all Disney bombast, a neon agreement that we all just step in line, accept the corporate smiley-face they'd pasted upon us. Be the stamped-out, pre-fab people they wanted us to be, going ooooh and ahhhh at every flickering firework designed to realign our brains.

There was a tourist photo booth near the corner of 47th and Broadway. Yolanda dragged her 67-year-old still-here carcass into it, passing the endless parade of gawking tourists and savvy street-dwellers. Slipping her last quarters in.

The second the camera clicked, she began to tear her own face off, one broken-nailed shred at a time. Her naked red skull the truest selfie she would ever take. Her screams, the purest sounds.

They all said she was crazy. And they were right.

But fuck if she didn't get her point across.

Z IS FOR ZENITH AND APEX

There is no bottom. And there is no top. That's the thing we have to wrestle with eternally. No matter how hard you fall, there is always a deeper darkness below.

But if that is true, there is also no end to the height and the light that a soul can aspire to. Up goes up forever, too.

A little perspective is a wonderful thing.

And that, my friend, is what splatterpunk means to me.

Intro to
THE MAN WHO FEARED THE SKY

This is less a story than a fable, I guess. Or maybe a parable, if you strip away believing in the madness.

It was not intended as a political statement. But looking back on it, I guess it can be read that way, too.

THE MAN WHO FEARED THE SKY

The blue didn't fool him. And the sun was a ruse, the clouds nothing more than puffy subterfuge. On the other side lay blackness and death, and there was nothing you could do to convince him otherwise. "It's called *space!*" he would holler at the walls of his room, as if they were the ones that needed convincing. "Look it up! It's in the dictionary, morons!"

I would say that his friends all thought he was crazy, but he didn't have any left, so that took care of that. For a minute and a half in the sands of time, he had a mildly amused internet following. But his insults were always the same, and the joke wore thin. When he went offline, with one last ugly tirade, there was almost no one left to notice or care.

He never went outside, of course.

Outside was where the sky was.

Inside, the walls were white, and the lights were always on. There were no windows, and no shadows, ever. He kept a light on under his bed, another aimed directly at him from the foot of it, lest the unseeable sneak beneath him. He had no covers, lest the darkness swallow his body while he fitfully slept. Naked, as always, because clothing did nothing but envelop you in menacing shade.

He never went outside, except in slumber: the one lightless space he could not control, no matter how much coffee he swallowed.

There would always come the time when his eyes would slide shut, those betraying folds of flesh unable to hold back any longer. Letting the darkness sink into his brain.

His dreams were filled with terror.

It was always the same, and never the same. He would stare at the door, and the door would stare back. Sometimes it opened. Sometimes it did not.

Sometimes there was light behind it, the way it was in waking life. A hallway, also lit to assassinate shadow, with no windows in sight.

In waking life, the only one who ever came to the door was the woman who brought him food and sundries: Maxwell House Coffee, Hormel Chili, Kellogg's Raisin Bran, Charmin Ultra-Soft, extra light bulbs. He didn't trust her, but relied on her nonetheless, curtly nodding from behind the door as she opened it, set the grocery bags inside, and pulled it shut decisively.

She never spoke -- he'd been quite clear about that -- in waking life. He had no interest in whatever she might have to say.

But in dreams, you never knew what would happen. In dreams, she spoke often. Sometimes in a voice he suspected was her real one, though he'd never heard it. Sometimes in voices that couldn't possibly be hers.

Sometimes it wasn't even her, but a masquerade of her, like the "blue sky" concealing the horror he knew awaited in the black beyond.

The worst was that, in dreams, he never knew what he was going to do. Sometimes there was no question. He ignored the voice, and the door closed, and he was alone again. Sometimes, they argued, and he summoned up the words he told himself over and over when awake, or shouted at the walls. Used them as fierce rebuttal to anything she/it threw back at him, the way voices and demons and the beckoning black cosmos always threw when they tried to lure him. Browbeat him. Pinch his every nerve. Suggest to him desires he refused to possess. Mock him for his cowardice and "fear of life".

Sometimes he would win those battles. Those were his favorite dreams.

In the worst of his dreams -- which came more and more frequently, as the years dragged on -- he had no control. The door would open, and he would feel himself helplessly moving toward it. No argument. No resistance. Will stripped from within.

Sleepwalking into the night.

It was never the same, but always the same. The lit corridor would go dark by degrees, and windows would erupt to either side, like stab wounds.

Then the sky would be there: a black rippling pool of infinitude, taunting him with its sparkles of illusory starlight. As if any light could survive there. As if there were any such thing as stars.

There was a skull at the core of the universe, floating in blackness. No sun. No moon. The world was as flat as a petri dish, and the hideous cosmos was the pair of black eyes that stared down upon him as the petri lid lifted. And lifted him helplessly up.

"I DEFY YOU!" he screamed, as the lie called gravity dragged him skyward nonetheless. Up through the illusion of stratosphere, stupid clouds like whispers of laughter that mocked him as he drifted up and up, until there was nothing but him and that cruel skull, confronting each other in the nightmare called space.

WHAT I WANT, said the skull, IS TO SEE THE LIGHT IN-SIDE YOU. SHOW ME, AND I WILL LET YOU GO FREE.

That was when the man who feared the sky had no words of rage or defiance left. Just the paralyzing fear.

I WILL OPEN YOU UP NOW, said the skull. And the light from the stars became skeletal claws, no longer pretending as they reached for his delicate skin, sliced it open from forehead to toe like the plastic film over a microwave dinner.

As his flesh peeled back, there were no organs within. No heart. And no light. Just a blackness as bottomless as the sky he despised.

AHHH, said the skull. YOU PUT OUT YOUR OWN LIGHT. SO DON'T TRY TO PIN IT ON ME, BABY.

YOU DID THIS TO YOURSELF.

Then his empty skinsuit fluttered free, a tattered flag of no man's nation, untethered from its pole and set adrift as his glittering eyes like stars bore witness...

At which point, he would scream. Awaken, alone. Inundated by incandescence entirely from without. And the cycle would begin again.

The man who feared the sky hated his dreams even more than he hated his painfully hollow life, which seemed to drag on for-ever. A tape loop so muddied and blurred by repetition that, by the end, the words he told himself no longer made sense even to him.

Then, one day, the woman stopped coming. A little while later, the supplies ran out. And the artificial lights, one by one, extinguished. First the bathroom, so he was forced to squat over the kitchen sink. Then the kitchen itself, and the foyer entrance, and the overheads of his bedroom abdicated their protection. Went dark. Slivering his world inch by inch, winnowing down to nothing, until even his walls disappeared.

His very last moments on Earth were spent huddled underneath his bed, by the last flickering light bulb. Cursing the darkness. Having learned not a thing.

Then the last bulb went out. And so did he.

While the sky went on and on and on.

Intro to
DON'T PUSH THE BUTTON

Sometimes, making art is a direct response to the moment at hand. In this case, a person in my personal life pissing me off so hard that I needed a place to put it, lest I lash out. And just make things worse than they were already.

It's funny that this became the title piece. But the second editor Christoph suggested it, the whole book came into focus. THANKS, CHRISTOPH!

DON'T PUSH THE BUTTON

I'm not pretty when I'm pushed
And you are pushing me now
Red lights flashing
Adrenaline up
Patience down
Your face a bullseye
Of concentric circles
I wanna flatten
Till the nostrils cave in

I don't like feeling this way
Work hard to avoid it
Do everything I can
Every chance I get
To defuse it with a laugh
A disarming smile
An honest attempt to listen
To see it from your side
To admit if I've done wrong
To meet you in the middle
Not take it personally
Let it roll off my back

But fuck if you're not
Pushing my button

I'm not pretty when I'm pushed

I tell you I'm sorry again
But it's getting harder to mean it
When you look at me like that
I see red
And it is like
A glimpse of the future
A future in which
I can't see red enough
And I won't be the only one
Seeing it, soon
If you don't back the fuck off
Right now

But you don't

My fist is a flower in reverse
Open petals closing
No time-lapse involved
Beyond the second it takes
To push your little
Button bullseye nose
All the way
To the back of your skull
And straight up
Into the gray

Then the screaming starts
And I go *not again*

But, yes, it's again
As you stagger back
As yet unaware
You are dead on your feet
As slow in demise
As you were your whole life
A dullard grown duller
In the last seconds left

The liquor store clerk
Goes for his phone
So much for the liquor store clerk
I vault over the counter
And take him down
And tell him I'm sorry
I'm sorry I'm sorry

But the future is red
And the future is now
And the only ones left
Who could possibly hear me
Are already out the door

And I'm thinking
I just wanted some beer
And a pack of smokes
I would have happily paid for
But now I take them
Take two, take three
Because fuck it
That camera just saw it all

And I wish that
You hadn't been such a prick
And I wish that
You hadn't cut in line
And I wish that
My whole life had been different
With a whole different person
As me

Then I get in the car
With the beer and the smokes
And the blood on my hands
And just drive again
Drive

Until the night
Of the strobing red
Catches up with me at last

Until that day
I swear to God
I will try to be nice
I will try to be patient

All I ask and I pray for
Over and over is
Please

Just don't push
My fucking button

I am sooooo
Not pretty that way

Intro to
IN THE WINTER OF NO LOVE

When I think about 2020, I think about the Sixties: a period of social upheaval and cultural revolt in which the events transformed not just the times, but the consciousness through which it was perceived. Mutating and evolving the brainscape forever.

The parallels to now are uncanny and instructive. It's a time I want to write about more.

But for now, this microcosmic psychedelic glimpse will have to do. And writing it was -- as all the hippies liked to say -- groovy.

IN THE WINTER OF NO LOVE

The street was a neon nightmare, a low-rent Disneyland of sleaze down which Marcie tromped in army boots. It was cold -- at least for California, with the chill November wind blowing in off the ocean -- and in her ankle-length coat of ratty fur, she felt like the least-naked woman on the strip.

All around her, the strip clubs, sex shoppes and movie theaters splayed posters of beautiful brazen women in their undergarments or less, the most revealing of them covering their nipples with their own hands, or somebody else's. Only three of them her.

It let her know where she stood in the pantheon of fuckability, if nothing else. And she rated pretty high, if you trusted the hungry hungry hippies sharing the sidewalk with her.

"Hey, baby. Hey, baby. You're bee--*yooooo*-teefull," crooned the scrawny black junkie at the corner, by the liquor store. He wasn't a pimp, but he sure dreamed of being one. She could see the glazed dollar signs in his eyes.

'Yeah," she said. "So what else is new?"

He laughed like that was the funniest thing he'd heard all night, though she bet he laughed like that all the time. She tried to imagine him before his idealism peeled off, if he ever had any at all. Then again, her own wasn't doing so hot these days, either.

Compassion, baby, she reminded herself. *Everybody's hurting out here.* Tonight, if nothing else, was all about the compassion.

In another world, things would have played out differently. In her dreams, they most certainly had. In her dreams, she kept her heart intact, and let her mind flow free.

But tonight, the red light was against her, so Marcie lit a smoke while she waited to cross, the cold wind blowing out three matches before she finally got it fired. She only had two packs of matches and five cigarettes left to get her through the night, until some moneyed gentleman or lady ponied up and bought her another day in paradise.

This was not the groovy San Francisco she'd dreamed of.

But it sure as shit was the one she got.

The sexual revolution was already decaying by the time Marcie made it to the free love capital of the world, in the summer of 1969. She had traveled a thousand miles times two, all the way from Milwaukee, Wisconsin, escaping the crew-cut legions of clueless men and finger-waggling helmet-haired Christian women who all wanted to call her a whore just because she loved to fuck, and was not ashamed of it.

She was only 16 in '67, when the actual Summer of Love went down. Two more years of high school before she could possibly break free. But she followed the news of the emerging rebellious youth culture mounting there, and more importantly, listened to the far-out sounds emanating from that mecca: The Grateful Dead, Quicksilver Messenger Service, Country Joe and the Fish's "Feel Like I'm Fixin' To Die".

She was particularly intrigued by Janis Joplin of Big Brother and the Holding Company, and Grace Slick of Jefferson Airplane: one flagrantly screaming out her naked love and need, in the most powerful terms possible; the other a mysterious witchy woman who spoke in code, but expressed her power not a speck less clearly.

Marcie wasn't sure which one she wanted to be -- a moot point, since she couldn't sing a note to save her life -- but she knew *where* she wanted to be. She wanted to be where the action was. She wanted to be part of changing the world. So the Monday after graduation, she packed her paisley rucksack with a couple changes of her hippest clothes, stole $137 bucks from her dad, wrote a goodbye note, and hit the highway thumb-first on her way to the west.

The first guy to pull over had a brand-new VW van with a GAS, GRASS, OR ASS - NOBODY RIDES FOR FREE bumper sticker slapped across its glove compartment. His name was Dewey, which pretty much described his eyes the second she got in the passenger seat. Even his long, scraggly ponytail popped a boner.

"Oh, wow," he said. "You look like Jane Asher. Or that movie star, Sharon Tate. Anyone ever tell you that?"

"Not since breakfast, baby." Cracking herself up with how easily those saucy words sprang to her lips. "So how far as you going?"

"How far are *you* going?" with a cuddly apelike leer.

"All the way to San Francisco, lover," she said. "It's gonna be groovy. You wanna come?"

And come he did, all the way across the country. She was low on gas and grass, but she had plenty of the third; and when he'd start to nod out at the wheel, sticking her hand in his pants always seemed to perk him up. In this way, they made it all 2,173 miles in just five days, with plenty of time in Dewey's optimistic little back-of-the-van love nest to make it worth everyone's while.

Dewey thought he was going to college in New Mexico, maybe joining a band, but she quickly changed his mind. His parents, of course, went out of their gourds. But if this was free love, he wanted waaaay more of that particular slice of the age of Aquarius.

When they landed in the Haight, second week of June, they thought they were in paradise. There was the Fillmore West, the Avalon Ballroom. All their favorite bands, performing nightly. And the streets were overflowing with colorful characters, psychedelic art, posters for protests and rallies and Be-Ins every which way they turned.

To see it all laid out before you like that, you'd think the war in Vietnam was really *going* to end. That equal rights for women and minorities was really *going* to happen. That you *could* reject Madison Avenue and the military/industrial complex, live a life that was simpler, more spiritual and free, less crawling with ancient dogma and narrow-minded dogshit.

But it didn't take long to figure out that they weren't the only people who came here without a plan. Because there was no plan. There was only a dream. And for every dreamer who landed even the smallest of happening gigs, there were six hundred others just wandering around, desperately hoping they could bum a next meal, talk someone into letting them crash at their pad, survive long enough to not give up and go back to their parent's basement in Ohio, or Vermont, or wherever the hell they came from.

Marcie and Dewey were able to keep finding overnight parking spaces while they sussed out the scene. But those spots were in increasingly scary neighborhoods. Pretty soon, they were spending more time in the Tenderloin than the Haight, watching middle-class creeps cruise for hookers in drag or otherwise, on their way in or out of pornographic clip shows and tittie bars.

Marcie being Marcie, it didn't take long for her to make friends, or something like them. The appetite for beautiful women was bottomless in *every* social circle, and she definitely ranked.

They found themselves invited to lots of parties, including orgies where she passed herself around first with gleeful abandon, then increasing discernment: learning who to screw just how and when, in order to get her foot in the door. And it wasn't like Dewey wasn't getting laid. Just not half as much as she was.

She landed a part-time job at a hip record store -- not enough to live on, but definitely enough to help -- and met tons of musicians breaking in from the margins. This was ostensibly good for Dewey, too, as he was pretty good on bass. And she was totally rooting for him.

The problem was he wasn't *that* good. Not enough to stand out in this incredibly competitive crowd, where originality was key.

Worse, he still thought he was her boyfriend.

That's when shit started to get weird between them.

"Which part of 'free love' don't you understand, Dewey?" she ranted, in one of their increasingly frequent arguments. " I came here to discover, and experience, and grow. Not to be dragged down."

"And I came here to be with you, Marcie!" he threw back. "That's what *you* don't understand!"

"Oh, baby," she said, pulling him close. "I'm with you right now, aren't I?" Then she put her tongue in his ear, which always made him weak-kneed, and they settled back down on his filthy mattress for a quick one that was far more sad than joyous.

Afterward, as she held him while the tears wore streambeds down his cheeks, he muttered, "I thought we came here to change the world. But the world's just changing us. And I don't like it."

She nodded and turned, lit a stick of incense, helplessly thinking there wasn't enough sandalwood and patchouli oil in the world to get the stink out of this van. And though it pained her deeply to admit it, that's when she knew they were coming to the end.

Better luck next life, she thought. And found herself wishing that next life would come a little sooner than later. Because this one was really starting to suck.

As the weeks dragged on, he had nothing but the money he increasingly begged from his parents, slowing to a trickle as their patience wore thin. Meanwhile, she found that stripping was a great, easy way to make quick cash. And when the opportunity to shoot a couple of scenes with some of the ladies came up, she was not about to ixnay $100 for fifteen minutes of going down on Mitzi or Darla. She was already doing that action for free.

The day after she found her own apartment, and did a cosmic three-way on acid with the drummer from Ultimate Spinach and a psychic healer named Wowza Majeur -- to which he was not invited -- Dewey found the needle in a parking lot with a passel of other smackhead losers. And that was that. Now he was needy on every level. And she just couldn't do it.

The day they broke up -- August 9th, one week before Wood-stock staged the last great gasp of the flower power generation -- was the day Sharon Tate was found murdered. Marcie came home to the sight of the front page story, taped to her door, with Tate's name crossed out and her own in its place. Beneath it, he had scrawled YOU'RE DEAD TO ME. And that was the last time they spoke.

It had been five months now since they landed, almost three since they'd seen each other. But when she heard he got a gig with the house band at some dive called The Shantyman, she figured she owed him at least this much.

Which brought her, at last, to The Shantyman's door. With the little sign out front that said:

TONITE!
BLACK SUNSHINE

There was a $3 cover, collected by the balding troll at the ticket kiosk. He licked his lips as he gave her change, let his gaze linger uncomfortably long. Pretty standard skeevy male chauvinist behavior. She rolled her eyes and strolled inside.

At first, she wasn't sure this could be the right place. The bartender looked to be at least 60, with a longshoreman's sense of pure rough trade style; and the three cackling cadavers holding court at the bar before him were equally antique. It looked more like her dad's VFW post in Milwaukee than anything she'd seen since she got to the Bay area.

But then the room opened up, and she saw the black light posters adorning the dark wood walls: Mr. Natural, Keep On Truckin', the obligatory dayglo peace symbol. It was pretty clear the owners of this dump had figured out no one wanted to hear Benny Goodman any more, made a few cheap concessions for the hippie demographic they needed if they wanted to keep the doors open.

But it didn't cover up the fact that, as hole-in-the-wall joints went, this one was pretty creepy. She could almost taste the history, and it didn't taste good. A quick peek at her watch said it was quarter to eleven. She figured she'd catch ten minutes of their set, then get the hell out of Dodge and back to the land of the slightly-more-living.

And that was when the band came on, with four drum stick clicks in the dark followed by a sonic boom: one half power-chord, one-half pre-recorded atomic blast, the Hiroshima mushroom cloud suddenly projected on the wall behind the stage.

Suddenly, she could see the members of Black Sunshine in stroboscopic silhouette. The gaunt, towering lead singer, swaying around the mic stand he clutched in one hand. Not exactly handsome, but snakily compelling nonetheless.

The guitarist and organist to either side weren't great lookers either. But the notes they hit were haunting on top of the hypnotic tom-tom trance state being laid down by the drummer, whose face remained hidden under a curtain of greasy bangs.

And, no fooling, there was Dewey on bass. He was staring at the floor, thudding out a sinuous pattern to the primal beat that didn't sound San Franciscan at all. More L.A. More like the fucking Doors, all dark and doomy. But pretty good. It suited the mood she was in, peace and love not having quite lived up to her expectations.

"Right on, Dewey," she muttered softly. "You sound good, baby. Good for you."

There were maybe forty people on the open dance floor, floating around like undersea creatures, getting their lethargic freak on under the strobing lights. People didn't dance together. They danced around each other. Sometimes eye-to-eye, but more often than not off in their own world.

Marcie wasn't judgmental. She liked to get super-high, too. Get into her own space. Let the spirit guide her. But there was something about the hollow-eyed emptiness in the faces of the people spinning around her that only reinforced The Shantyman's sketchy-ass vibe.

These were the people who had fallen off the fringes of the fringe. The castoffs of the countercultural revolution, far more narcotic than psychedelic. Bottom-feeders, with no bottom left to feed on. The lostest of the lost.

For the second time, she felt the urge to leave. But the music was powerful, growing more so by the second. And like a train wreck in the making, she wanted to see what happened next. It was definitely not the weirdest scene she'd stumbled into, or ever would, if she was lucky.

She wondered who had some pot, at least. Started scoping out likely suspects as she steered her way to the front.

The further in she went, the toastier the room got with unwashed body heat, so she opened her jacket, revealed her coochie-high skintight pink velvet micro-mini dress. It was one of Dewey's favorites, and she wasn't sure whether it was to torture him or reward him. But it glowed in the black light, and strobed in-between. One fact was for certain: it was made to be seen.

The lead singer spotted her first, raised a hungry eyebrow before suddenly remembering it was time to croon. He cast a gaze back at Dewey, with a knowing grin.

And then, at last, began to sing:

> It's dark tonight
> In the winter of no love
> All the stars you came to shine with
> Are not glittering above
> And, oh, your disappointment
> It just fits you like a glove
> What's so easy
> Makes you queasy
> In the winter of no love

In the time it took for that verse to flow through, she felt the gentle push of the crowd from behind. They were moving slowly toward the stage, mesmerized by the throbbing groove and his rich, deep baritone voice. She, too, was starting to move with the rhythm, the intoxicatingly persuasive syncopation.

And when a pasty-faced scarecrow in a Nehru jacket passed a doobie her way, she gratefully accepted, took a long toke, passed it back. He nodded, unsmiling, returned his gaze to the band.

By the time she exhaled, it was already too late.

Suddenly, the room seemed to skew sideways in all directions at once, as her vision went fisheye. Her brain and the floor turned to mud, the strobing lights like pulsars flaring numbly within.

Ooooooh noooo went a voice she barely recognized as her own, as the angel dust took effect. She didn't know what PCP was, but she knew what it was doing, elephant-tranquilizing her as surely as a dart to the neck.

She stumbled back as if to fall, but the press of bodies kept her upright, rubberband limbs all but useless as her gaze bleared toward the stage.

And Dewey was looking at her now, face mutating as the world went wrong, his eyes black holes that glittered redmeat red at on/off intervals. His sharkmouth crawled up either cheek in a grin too huge for comprehension, his fishbelly creme bass bending and writhing in crotchulous undulation.

And as his fuzzed-out bass notes hammered through her bones, she felt the call of the walls, the floor and ceiling, as sure as the words now being chanted by the band.

All you who are lost
Belong to us
All you who are lost
Belong to us

Something tore inside her bowels, like a menstrual cramp only higher, and seemingly farther away. She vaguely felt wetness run down her legs, wasn't sure if she was peeing or bleeding. There was a hand holding her up by the right shoulder. Its fingers runnelled down the front of her coat like fatty wax.

And her vagina filled with something thick as cock, with none of the pleasure.

From within.

All you who are lost

Belong with us

In the winter of no love

Marcie screamed as her lower intestines crawled out of her holiest of holes and out into the room, waggling blindly wormlike, curling toward the sound. She felt herself emptying, screamed again, reeling back against the wall of bodies.

But they were already melting, too. Bodies sagging, as faces dripped. A bouillabaisse of rotten squalor, giving themselves up at last to the only place that would have them.

Being claimed by this hellhole, and Black Sunshine.

Now she knew why they were the house band.

Marcie toppled on top of a sloe-eyed blonde whose eyes oozed out to either side. Her slick hand grazed Marcie's cheek before its arm dissolved into the floor.

Then came the onslaught of lead guitar, every raw treble note a rivet driving itself into her flesh. It tried to pin her, but she crawled with all her might, finding strength through fury. Going I will not die like this.

The next body she met was already liquified but for the skull, which crumbled like a candy shell. She clawed past it, felt her fingernails snap as she grabbed the wooden floorboards, felt the floorboards grab back. Ancient mouths with thick splinter teeth, opening up to sample, bite, and suck her in.

She screamed again: a wail somehow strangely in tune with the music that assailed her. The most in-tune her voice had ever been. And that scared her most of all.

There is no other
Place for you
Will be no other
Trace of you
Come wallow in
The waste of you
Come on
Come on
COME ON!
COME ON!

She could not look back over her shoulder. She could not look back over her shoulder. She did not want to see her guts slide across the floor behind her, moving inexorably toward the stage. She did not want to see the triumph in Dewey's eyeless eyes as his own dark umbilicus crawled out his ass and down his stupid bell-bottomed pants leg in an attempt to fuse with hers.

And she was emptying. Yes, she was. Belly concaving to the ribcage, the spine, as more and more of her squeezed then squirted out her pussy and into the room. There was no question that she was dying now. The only question was where.

The door was a trillion more than 2,173 miles away, but she knew it when she saw it, crawling past the bar, where the Shantyman regulars cawed like vultures, having seen this all before. Placing bets on how far she'd get. Eyes black as Satan's coal.

But she was not going back. She was going forward, one desperate lunge at a time. The music still huge, but receding as an angry honking cabbie drove by, honk like the voice of God saying you know who you are, you know who you are.

There was no troll at the door. No cover charge on life. She saw headlights, heard voices through the floating rectangular slab as the miles turned to inches turned to nothing turned to there...

...and her lungs pulled her still-beating heart down and down, toward the blackness beyond...

And then there was light. Amazing light.

The color of which she had only dreamed.

Her face was at rest upon green, green grass. Every filament bright, in the warm starlight. An infinite plane of glowing.

With a pair of hooves, stopping just an inch from her face.

"Hey," said a voice. "It's okay now. It's okay."

She blinked, looked up, fisheyed no longer as the black numbness shuddered out of her in a wave.

"What?" she said to the satyr who loomed above her: shirtless, hairy, not remotely scary, with a goatlike psychedelic glimmer in his eye that liked and loved and knew her in a flash, beneath his wild hair and great flowing horns.

"You don't ever wanna go in there," he said. "That's not why you came."

Marcie shook her head to clear it, not to disagree. Somewhere in the enormous distance, the last whimper of Black Sunshine echoed off to nothingness. Like they were never there. Like they never mattered at all.

"Where am I?" she said.

"Where you always wanted to be," he said. "And all you have to do is let go."

"Right." As she helplessly started to cry.

"Release your attachments."

"Oh, God…"

"Forgive yourself."

Choking. "I am so sorry I hurt him…"

"Aw, sugar. It happens. Just don't do it again, if you can help it," he said. " You'll get better with practice, okay? That's what we get whole lives for. Lives upon lives upon lives."

"OH, GOD!" As her cord to the world, the dimension she once knew gut-snapped at last. But her heart still with her. Her spirit intact.

"The world you want may take decades or centuries to happen, back there," he said. "But it's already happening here, forever. This is where you're going. This is where the best of you, the soul of you, has always been. We all know how cool you are, and how well you mean, and how beautiful you will always be, even if you come back ugly in disguise. Because that's how the game is played."

It was the most perfect thing he could possibly have said, all infinity flowing before and beyond them.

"So where's the party?" she asked, grinning, as he helped her to her feet.

"Up here," he said. "And I think you're gonna like it. Rumor has it you're a fucking firecracker."

"You better believe it, lover," she purred into his ear. Stuck her tongue in. Made him weak in the knees.

As winter turned to summer once again.

Intro to
SKINNY MINNIE

Every once in a while, someone will send me a picture. Say "WRITE A STORY ABOUT THIS!" And sometimes I do.

SKINNY MINNIE

You'd think she'd be fatter, given how much she fucking eats. Chained to the table. Doing almost nothing but.

But when what's left of Don's head lands on the plate before her, with his lushly-crested pate already lopped off at mid-forehead, Skinny Minnie digs right in. It's like cranium souffle, or brains tartar. Were she capable of happiness, I would say this is it. Every morsel an unparalleled treat.

The drugs don't seem to be hurting, either, at least in terms of keeping her focused. A little injection goes a long, long way.

And she has a long, long way to go.

Never thought of myself as a big-on-revenge guy. That always seemed like a lower emotion. But now that I know just how low we can go, it seems downright borderline uplifting. Like there couldn't be a better fucking use of my time, here in our last days left.

The attic of Don's never-too-occupied skull empties out quickly in her two-clawed assault, Minnie licking her fingers when the bowl is empty, then ripping away at the plump, juicy cheeks. I hope she remembers not to pop those peepers, though the bowl we're reserving for her desert is overflowing already. So many mocking eyes to meet.

You never think of how many people have hurt you until you line them all up and kill them, one by one.

And you never feel like justice has been done until the one who wronged you wrongest has to sin-eat them all. And love it.

Oh, Skinny Minnie. You're a much better zombie than you ever were a human.

Eat up, baby. Eat up.

Intro to
TENDRILS FOR DAYS

I don't think Jesus and Chthulhu hang out nearly often enough.

TENDRILS FOR DAYS

"If there is no God," demanded Todd, "then who's to stop me from doing whatever I want?"

The thing strapped to the table couldn't answer: Holy Bible crammed between its mandibles, duct-taped so tight it couldn't chew its way through.

All its squiggling tentacled limbs had been lopped, which took some doing. It kept growing new ones. And every eyeball he popped was replaced by another. Soulless. Unblinking. Staring him down, even as it writhed in agony.

"Don't you look at *me* like that, demon spawn!" Todd hollered, drunk and teetering. "You can't infect me with your mind-beams! Because God IS real! Christ is real! And only through His grace am I delivered from my sins!"

There were more tendrils growing, so he picked up the weed-whacker and once again applied it to the monster's bulbous torso, wetly shaving the growth away. This was better than knife or saw. Less squirting black goo on his hands.

Todd hated the fact that it didn't scream. The screams were what he loved the most. But it would not give him the satisfaction. No shame. No penitence. No pleas for forgiveness or mercy.

He put down the weed-whacker and picked up the bottle, which was running low. But the bourbon dulled the itching all over his body. And Jesus had no problem with wine. *This is my blood*, Jesus said.

The problem was that the monster wouldn't die. God knows he'd tried. Bisecting the brainpan should have done it, sneaking up from behind with hatchet in hand. And its rigorously hacked-open innards were now a buzzing buffet for swarms of more conventionally-sized insects. The kind he'd been ripping the wings from since *he* was a child.

But still it squirmed, on his Table of Submission. Where so many little girls had gone before. And he could not cut enough to make it fit his Procrustean bed.

"DON'T TEMPT ME, DEMON!" howled Pastor Todd, as the thing's insectile anus undulated, and the first pale hairs of his forearms thickened and lengthened, jutting out of his shrieking skin.

Then it was his turn to scream.

The blank eyes said nothing. Only stared and stared, as Todd's entire body convulsed and erupted, flesh tearing open from everywhere at once. So many throbbing protuberances. Each more wrong than the last.

There would be no more whacking. And Jesus be damned.

We're talking tendrils for days.

Intro to
SKIPP'S SELF-ISOLATING ABC'S OF THE
COVID-19 (STAGE ONE)

When Covid first struck, I was paralyzed in terms of writing about it. The topic was just too huge. And I had no idea how it would end. (As of this writing, I still don't!)

But then a couple of maskless assholes in a grocery store made me realize that the story could only be told in a kaleidoscope of tiny moments. That I couldn't say everything. But that I could say a lot of little somethings. And that if they added up to even a fraction of the sum of their parts, that might be good enough for me.

Insofar as I know, it's the only piece of fiction the writing website LitReactor ever posted online: not as a "look at me", but as a potential template for other people to share their fragments of the enormity. Still no word as to whether anyone else took me up on the challenge. But you do what you can.

And, honestly, I suspect there will be no shortage of pandemic stories by the time this book comes out. So we're probably fine.

SKIPP'S SELF-ISOLATING ABC'S OF THE COVID-19 (STAGE ONE)

A IS FOR AMAZON PRIMATE

Amy waits on the porch, as she often does these days. Just her and her phone, a bottle of whiskey she's been hitting since 10:00 ayem, her pack of American Spirit Blues, and a folding chair beside her folding table, where her ashtray sits in a state of perpetual overflow.

Somehow, the day has stretched till 2:00. Sun high in the sky, but not half as high as she is. She sings along to Lana Del Rey's "Born to Die", not caring how badly. There's no one on the street to hear her. The streets are empty in this neck of the woods, on the outskirts of suburbia. Barely a car in an hour or more.

Oh, Andy, she thinks. *Please tell me you're comin' soon.*

Ordinarily -- for the last five years -- she'd be waiting tables at the Delta Bar and Grill. Serving Shrimp and Grits Benedict and a Bloody Mary to some lucky fellow, sober as a judge herself. Now she lives in terror that she'll never see the Delta again without a "Closed" sign out front.

Not that she'll be seeing that any time soon. She's too scared to take public transportation. Too scared to walk more than the ten looooong blocks to the nearest liquor store and 7-11. Too scared to do much of anything but drink and wait for Andy's beat-up Toyota to arrive.

And then, lo and behold, it appears in the distance. Two blocks away and closing. She lets out a cheer, takes a celebratory swig, starts to stumble to her feet, decides against it. She is made of numb, but she's not dumb.

So she waits until he actually pulls up out front before getting up. Waving hi. Pulling up her mask.

And then tumbling, face-first, down the two steps from her porch to the unforgiving sidewalk below.

"OH, JESUS, LADY!" he hollers, muffled through his own face mask, slamming his car door shut as he races toward her, then stops twelve feet away. He wants to help her. Is not sure how. Maintaining distance is his only defense.

She lets out a scream that turns into laughter before descending into tears that mix with the blood flowing down her forehead. Not just drops. A cascade.

"OOPS!" Amy says, laughing again, pulling herself half-up and waving him away. "I'm fine! I'm fine! Thank you!"

What she wants is for him to pick her up from the pavement. What she wants is for him to wipe the blood from her face, peel his mask back, and kiss her. What she wants is to take him inside and fuck him senseless. Not feel so alone anymore. Thank him for risking his life for her, every time he makes this trek. Brings her groceries. Saves her life. Is her hero.

But that's now how it is, so that's not gonna happen. As she struggles to her feet, embarrassed. And he, equally embarrassed, just unloads her boxes of food that will keep her alive for the next week at least. And hopes her relief check comes in. So she can send for him again.

Maybe someday, she will get her wish.

Cuz, frankly, Andy would like that, too.

B IS FOR BULLSHIT AND BEAUTY BOTH

"Okay," Bea says. "So let me get this straight. It's 5G cell phone signals. It's Chinese biological warfare, waged on America. It's American biological warfare, waged on the Chinese. Bill Gates did it. Or the Democrats did it. Or Satan did it. Or it isn't even really happening at all."

"Always with the mouth," her father snaps from a thousand miles away. *"Always the one with all the answers."*

"I'm not saying I know the answers," she says. "I'm saying I don't. And you don't, either."

"I just know what I'm told."

"Yeah, by Fox News!" She can hear it blaring in the background, as they speak.

"It's better than the lies from CNN!"

"Dad, I don't like CNN much more than you do."

"Or what do they call it? MSDNC."

"Oh, that's a hoot. Okay, I like Rachel Maddow."

"Of course you do. She's a lesbian, too."

"Well, there's that. But, you know, she does actual research. She doesn't just spout off the top of her head. Regardless. I agree she was in Hillary's pocket. I'm still working on forgiving her for that."

A moment of silence, from the other end of the phone. She lets him savor that victory, is glad this isn't a video call.

"The point is, something is going on. And it's killing people all over the world. Not just in America. It's a global pandemic. The key word is global."

"Well, where did it come from then?" he demands. "It wasn't here last year! It didn't just sprout out of thin air!"

"Well, here's an idea," she says, as a light goes off behind her eyes. "I didn't hear it on corporate media. I'm just making it up as I go along. So the polar ice caps are melting."

"*Aw, Christ Almighty.*"

"No, seriously. They are. You don't have to believe in global warming. Maybe Jesus just does it with his loving hands."

"*Bea.*"

"Hang on. Point is, we can both agree that Antarctica and the Arctic Circle are the coldest places on Earth, right?"

"*Right.*"

"They've been frozen since the dawn of time. At least since the dinosaurs. You still love dinosaurs, right?"

His voice softens. "*I taught you to love dinosaurs.*"

"Yes, you did." Smiling. She really does love her dad. "So let's talk about the ice that's been sitting up there for the last million years or whatever. Okay? If it's starting to melt -- for whatever reason -- that means that things that have been buried there for a million years might be coming to the surface. Asleep all this time."

"*Huh.*" He pauses again. She can almost see him thinking. The Alzheimer's is wearing him down, but she remembers the inquisitive mind that raised her, 46 years ago.

"For all we know, the diseases that killed off every species before us are just waking up now. They're not new. They're incredibly old. Even older than you, Dad!"

He laughs. "*My little smarty-pants.*"

"So what if the Coronavirus was just waiting for us, all this time? Not from a lab. Not from anyone's government conspiracy. And if it's the Devil? You always said that the Devil was patient."

"*But these are the End Times.*" With evangelical gravity.

"Maybe they are, and maybe they aren't. But these are these times. So we do what we can. You wear a mask when you go out, right?"

"*Mom does. I don't go out at all. My knees.*"

"I know." Like the arthritis wasn't enough. "But she's alright, right? Is she home?"

"*She's napping. She sleeps like a rock. She's a rock.*"

"I know."

"*You know she loves you, right, baby?*"

"Always has, always will. I know the drill." Wiping away a tear.

"*And I love you, too.*"

"I love you sooooo much."

Her dad never used to cry out loud, even the slightest bit. That was her job. But there's something beautiful in hearing him yank back a sob, much as it saddens her. His heart opening in these private moments, even as his mind shuts down.

"*Okay, then,*" he says, reigning it back in.

"I'll call back on Wednesday, okay?"

"*God willing.*"

"God better."

They both laugh.

And, with that, say good night.

C IS FOR COUGHING IN PUBLIC CUZ YOU THINK IT'S FUNNY

Here's a joke: three goons walk into a Safeway. Strapping 20-somethings from the jocular white jock end of the gene pool. No masks. No nothing. Not a care in the world.

To be fair, only 87% of the people in the supermarket are wearing them. And most of the ones that aren't maybe just don't have one, and aren't sure how to make one. Or they did, but the straps broke. Or they're socially isolating so much that they think they can get away with a quick ten minutes, shopping scrupulously, and then getting the hell out.

Carl knows the drill. He resisted wearing a mask for the first six weeks, mostly because he started smoking at the age of eight, and he's 68 now, and it was fucking hard to breathe through the fabric. Still is. But he finally broke down, sawed a t-shirt in half, and turned it into a bandanna he could pull up only when he spoke with somebody, and leave off in the mostly-empty aisles between. It makes him feel like a bandito, which is kind of fun. So he's rolling with that.

Carl's at the Chinese food counter by the deli, where they're still serving up fresh batches of General Tsao's Chicken and Mandarin Beef with noodles and/or fried rice. It's nice to have a hot meal cooked by someone else sometimes, when you're all alone. Order two, and you could eat for three days.

He's standing six feet back from the counter, staring through the glass at what he wants. Waiting for the nice lady to get done taking a deli order from a large black woman with smiling eyes and her tiny daughter, wearing matching tiger-stripe masks.

The three goons saunter up to the deli counter, and instantly surround the woman and child. One moves straight up to the glass, immediately starts poking his fingers at various items. Smearing his fingerprints as he goes along. He has curly red hair. Carl dubs his Curly.

"Hey!" he says, yelling over his shoulder. "You want Pepper Jack or White American?"

"I want allllll that dark meat," says the big-nosed one he dubs Larry. He is rubbing his hands lovingly across the glass, like he's trying to give it a massage.

And that leaves Moe, the tallest of the three. Standing barely a foot behind the woman and her kid. Very deliberately doing so, to the point that she takes a long stride forward, dragging her child along tersely. Closer than she wants to the others now triangulating her.

Then Moe coughs. Extravagantly. Sprayingly. Directly into the back of the woman's head. Not even lifting an elbow to stop it.

"I GOT THE COVID!" he bellows, as she recoils in horror. And the trio erupts with laughter.

"Oh, you sons of bitches," Carl mutters, backing up from the counter, pulling up his bandanna, even though he's thirty feet away. Particulates travel. That's the whole fucking point.

He will not be ordering from here today. And is gladder than usual he didn't start shopping first, so he has no basket to selfishly abandon.

He heads straight down the nearest aisle, full of frozen entrees he might have grabbed. Walks fast, determined, rounds the end of the aisle, walks down two more, and then heads back up front, where he sees the crying woman and child fleeing. Hears the guffaws still ringing, as the shit-talk rings.

Most of the people in this store have no idea what just happened. A Vietnamese couple going out the exit look nervously up, then down at their feet. Carl moves toward them, keeping a safe distance from everyone.

He parked at the far left of the parking lot, by the gas station, five or six spots down. The homeless by the dumpster are paying him no mind. He opens the back of the pickup truck, heads straight for his tools, the screwdriver he needs.

Removes his license plate. Tosses it in the back. Screws in a new one quick. Out-of-state, but up to date.

By the time he's done, the mother has almost strapped her kid into the passenger seat, both of them sobbing. "I'M SORRY YOU CAN'T SIT ON MY LAP! But soon as we get home, oh, baby…!"

Carl steps into the front seat, slams the door, revs the engine. Doesn't need to make that much noise, but can't help himself. It fucking revs him up to do it.

Carl is a war vet. A lifelong Republican. Hopes he gets his party back someday. Hopes he gets his life back.

But he knows an enemy combatant when he sees one.

He pulls into reverse, idles to the side, pointed backwards, watches the exit. Is delighted to see the three hollering goons escorted out by Safeway security staff, in his rearview mirror. It pains him to see how scared the staffers are. And how completely unrepentant are these stooges, as they strut triumphant. Directly toward him.

The second the staffers are back inside, and it's just those assholes, Carl stomps on the gas.

The look on their faces is priceless.

The funniest thing they ever did.

Carl takes side-streets for the whole five minutes it takes for him to get back to his garage. There's a tense moment, when a cop car comes the other way. But they just keep driving, and so does he. They got other shit to do.

It isn't hard to fix the fender, hose the blood off the bumper, tires, and undercarriage. Mostly tires and undercarriage, cuz he speed-bumped those motherfuckers thrice before tearing ass off into the street.

He will never forget that mother's smile.

And hopes to god the EMTs have the PPE they need for this particularly messy cleanup on aisle three.

D IS FOR DEAD ON ARRIVAL

In times of plague, you don't always have time to test the already deceased. You just assume they have it. Even if they got run over by a pickup truck three times.

During ordinary flu season, a lot of people die from the flu. But just because they had the flu doesn't mean that's what they died from. That heart attack, that brain embolism, had been building up for years. The timing's just coincidence.

Point being that we'll never know how many people this shit takes out. People die every day.

But if you don't think people are really dying from this, ask the people who are watching it happen every day, as they try to save them.

The next life they save might be your own.

E IS FOR "IT'S THE ECONOMY, STUPID!"

Eric is rich as sin. But that could change at any second, his broker explains, as they watch the stocks tumble together.

In the 1920's, when the market collapsed, it was not uncommon for the *nouveau-riche* to go from "Top of the world, Ma!" to the bottom of the skyscraper where they just jumped out the window with a splat. There are few fortunes that can't turn on a dime. And Eric's is turning fast.

Eric's also concerned that the poor might eat him. Plow through the gates of his gated estate. Overwhelm security, no matter how well-armed. Bust down his door. And tear him limb from fucking limb, toss his carcass on the backyard barbeque, while alternately ransacking the place, murdering his family, and doing cannonballs off the diving board of his super-sweet Vegas swimming pool.

It's hard to be hated by 99.9% of the world. Especially when you depend on them to keep hitting your casinos. A sucker is born every minute, yes. But when they all go broke, or start dying at once...

...and when yours are the vectors for a massive reinfection that spreads across all fifty states, and every country in the civilized world, that whole world now cursing your name...

They say the house always win. But now the house is crumbling. He took a gamble on reopening. And nobody won.

"You might want to consider shutting down for good," his broker says, "and putting what's left offshore. Cuz you are running out of choices fast."

And that's when the gates break down.

And the hungry hordes pour in.

F IS FOR FUCKING UP

Freddy was fine, until three days ago, when the symptoms crept up and caught him. Now he's on a gurney in a hallway without end. Gurney after gurney. Lined up. And amen.

And he finds himself going, *how the fuck did this happen? I WAS SO CAREFUL. What was my mistake?* Pouring over every second of the last two weeks. Every surface touched. Every item of food purchased, wiped down before it even hit the kitchen counter or fridge. Every piece of mail, or bill of currency exchanged.

Freddy's OCD had kicked in well before the Covid hit. He'd been washing his hands forty times a day since he was a teen. He felt naturally predispositioned for the clampdown. Had spent his whole life training.

On the one hand, it just seems so unfair. On the other, he must have done something. Some chink in the armor that somehow slipped through. Replaying it over and over, as he coughs into his mask. A chorus of coughs, all up and down the corridor. In a hospital with no end. And no available ventilators.

He brings one hand up to wipe his itching eye. Catches himself, too late.

And remembers.

G IS FOR GIVING UP THINGS

Gigi misses kissing strangers. Gary misses baseball games. Georgia misses college classes, not to mention parties. Gertude misses her great-grandchildren.

Gioseppo misses naked artist models. Gina misses posing for him. Greg misses telling people what to do, and lording it over. George misses telling Greg to eat shit.

Gretta gave up on the world a long time ago, wishes the rivers clean. Gogo is giving up professional wrestling for now, but cannot wait to grapple again.

Grace is giving up everything but grace itself.

God is watching.

Gerry ain't giving up nothing. That's just how he rolls.

H IS FOR HELPING EACH OTHER

The only thing that makes sense right now.

I IS FOR I DON'T GIVE A SHIT

The only thing that doesn't.

J IS FOR JACKING OFF

Love and desire got to go somewhere. When there's no one to touch, you touch yourself.

News out of China says coronavirus might linger in the sperm, even if you survive it. No word as yet as to whether it's sexually contagious. One guesses lady-juices might behave (or misbehave) the same way. Every horny human of every persuasion wants the answer to that.

J is also for "Jesus, I hope I get to ever fuck again."

K IS FOR KRISTA, ON HOLD FOREVER

Kevin awakens at 8:00 ayem to the sound of treacly saxophone, on a bed of wilted muzak, wafting up from the back porch below. He groans. *Dear God, not this again.*

Fifteen minutes later, he drags himself downstairs, having heard it exactly fifteen more times. Their home is a bureaucratic waiting room from Hell now. If Satre's *No Exit* had a soundtrack, it would certainly be this.

He doesn't blame the State Unemployment Bureau for the waiting time. With 36-plus million newly unemployed, he knows those poor bastards on the other end of the line are overburdened beyond imagining. Doing God's work, government-style. God knows he and Krista need those checks.

But after eight hours in limbo yesterday, he holds Satan personally responsible for the muzak. It's a brutalizing onslaught of sonic tedium, ostensibly designed to soothe, with a secret agenda of rendering one helpless in the process of completely obliterating the human soul.

Krista is a concert violinist, her symphony orchestra in limbo, her junior high school teaching gig on hold as indefinitely as she. So it's a trillion times worse for her, he knows. He's just a gym coach who happens to hate shitty music. Love's funny like that.

He makes her an omelet and a fresh cup of coffee before venturing out to the porch. Sees her staring into the middle distance, phone in hand. Like holding it will make it end faster.

"How you doin', my baby?" he asks.

"I haven't felt this suicidal since I was thirteen," she says. "But thank you. I love you."

The bad news is, they have to listen to that muzak 80,000 more times.

The good news is, the checks eventually arrive.

L IS FOR LYFT, LIFE, AND DEATH

How many times can you spray your car with disinfectant before it will never stop smelling like disinfectant again? Lynn's pretty sure she's about to find out. Praying every time that it works, as she wipes down the seats and door handles, the steering wheel, then sprays the trunk. And leaves the windows perpetually open. At least a crack, even in the pouring rain.

But people still need rides. And she still needs money. Hardly ever to the airport anymore, which is great. She will not pick up from there. But just locally getting from here to there has become a thing, as public transport turns into a petri dish, even more so than ever before.

Case in point: she pulls into the mostly-dead strip mall, one Rite-Aid, Petco, and Grocery Outlet away from the apocalypse. Gym dead. Pizza joint dead. Coffee shop dead. Thai restaurant dead. Hair and nail joint dead. Nobody's getting Lotto tickets from Lulu right now.

But the lady waving from the curb as she pulls up is sketchy as hell. No mask, for starters. Yelling into her phone, as strike two. Junkie skinny for thirds.

"Nope," Lynn says, moving on. "Like I'm dyin' for you, bitch."

The next one is just fine, and tips her two dollars on a four-dollar run, gives her a great review. "Thank you for making me feel safe," the lady says. "You don't know how much that means."

Lynn thanks her back, watches her go. Gets out. Wipes the door, the handles, the seat. Sprays like her life depends on it.

And hopes she still has this job tomorrow.

M IS FOR MISSING YOU

"It's been three months," Monica says. Marcus sighs, says he knows. Says he's aching for her. Knows he means it. She is aching for him, too.

It's not like he's a thousand miles away. It's exactly one hundred and forty-seven blocks, as the crow flies carless.

If there was one thing they ever swore to each other -- in the ups and downs of their complicated, non-monogamous poly-sexual relationship -- it was that they would keep each other safe. Would not endanger each other. Biologically, at least. (Both have pre-existing conditions that coronavirus could steer directly to death.) Would not feed each other disease. Careful. Careful. Always careful and wild.

But when polygamy whittles down to monogamy, then non-agamy at all, the choices refine in startlingly clarifying ways.

"I miss them all," she says.

"Me, too."

"But you're the one," she says.

And so they wait.

N IS FOR NOT NOW, SWEETHEART

Ned doesn't know how many times he has to beat Nellie, just to get her to shut up. Has already hidden every sharp or blunt object he can find.

But it's getting harder and harder to fall asleep, even with her down on the couch and the bedroom door locked.

O IS FOR OPINIONS

They're the things we fall back on when we don't know what the fuck we're talking about. Which is to say, we fall back on them all the time.

I'd like to suggest that we're emotional creatures first, and intellectual creatures maybe third or fifth. Which is to say that we feel things, then attempt to put words to them. Or better yet, let other people put words to them. If we like the words, that becomes our new expressed opinion.

It's astounding how much time we spend, just squirting other people's opinions at each other, then responding emotionally to any disagreement as if it were not just a personal but a physical attack. Then personally attacking that person in kind, and escalating that shit out of all proportion to the actual regurgitated ideas that were never even ours to begin with.

In the last years of her life, my mom and I made a deal. We could discuss any and everything under the sun, so long as we did not invoke political pundits. We restricted the conversations of controversial topics to how we actually felt, in person-to-person encounters from our lives, instead of dragging in opinionators. And honest to God, we never argued again. We disagreed sometimes. But we agreed more often than not, on purely human terms.

It was one of the best decisions I ever made.

So basically, fuck opinions. Yes, we're all entitled to them, like the half-baked and equally hallucinatory egos they rode in on. Both are phantoms, hijacking truth. When the truth is the only thing that actually matters.

But, of course, that's just my opinion.

P IS FOR PAN-TASTIC

Pablo wins the poker game again. If anybody had real money, he'd be king of the underpass.

Instead, he's just another homeless guy sitting around a packing crate with four other homeless people, their tents or whatever they have behind them. There's a roaring trash barrel fire. It's 4:30 in the morning. A dozen others are trying to sleep.

"But here's the thing," Pablo says, grinning, as Peter scoops up the cards. "Yeah, we're all in the shit right now. But the deck just got shuffled by the Covid, okay? Those jobs we lost? They're gonna come back. It just won't be the same people. Maybe next time, we're the ones with the better jobs!"

"What if they don't open back at all?" This from Paula, whose life is a frown.

"The restaurants might not be the same restaurants. But people still gotta eat, right? So somebody else reopens under a different name. It's still the same cards in play. You know? THE WHOLE DECK JUST GOT SHUFFLED. The whole world just got shuffled. And nobody knows how it's gonna land yet. But it's the same fucking world. And I am going to play it. So you gonna deal those fucking cards now or what?"

Peter shuffles and deals a round of Five Card Stud, with a baleful eye that reminds Pablo that this guy hates him right now more than death. Pablo's optimism a personal affront.

Somewhere around dawn, Peter will attempt to slit his throat while he sleeps, and Pablo will beat him within an inch of his life, kicking his ass all the way down to the riverbed and into the water, yelling, "Hope you know how to swim, motherfucker!"

But for now, he nods at his pair of aces.

And looks forward to the rest of the new hand he's dealt.

Q IS FOR QUARANTINE FEVER

These four walls
  Are the jowls of Satan
  Closing in
  As I howl and spin

R IS FOR RESET, AGAIN AND AGAIN

When your only connection to the outside world is an internet
modem that shuts down every fifteen minutes -- unplugging,
replugging, ad infinitum -- it helps to remember that you're lucky
as fuck to have one in the first place.

They're shipping a new one, Renee! It should be here on
Monday.

First world problems, indeed.

S IS FOR BOTTOMLESS SORROW

Two of Sadie's mom's best friends passed away on Sunday. One
after another, like bowling pins. Different nursing homes. Same
result.

Both so kind, when her own mother passed three weeks ago.
A whole older generation, succeeding in ever-more-rapid waves of
pandemic spread.

Sadie is running out of senior citizens to fear for, or love in real
time. The sorrow is huge.

She looks to her children, and says, "I swear to God, we will
survive."

T IS FOR THE TOTALITY

We tend to forget this is all one world. Wherever you are, it's not just happening there. It's happening everywhere.

I don't know how many Eskimos are currently dying from the coronavirus. But one is one too many. Meanwhile, refugee camps all over the globe are helpless breeding grounds for the disease. Every city a potential hot spot. And every small town only needs one careless or unwitting fuckup to spread to the next one. The next one. Then you.

If it's happening anywhere, it's happening everywhere, sooner or later.

TAG! YOU'RE IT!

U IS FOR UNIVERSAL HEALTH CARE

Under the circumstances, this shouldn't even be a fucking question anymore.

V IS FOR VA-VA-VOOM

Vivian is crazy-hot. And Victor ain't nothin' to sneeze at, himself. That's what the masks are for.

But as they pass on the street, eyes the only visible parts of their faces, they instantly know they were meant to meet as meat. Then breed. With future offspring to feed.

There are gonna be a ton of new babies, is all I'm sayin'.

W IS FOR "WHY, GOD? WHY?"

Wendy prays on her knees for an answer, alone. Wendell assures his parishioners that if they gather together, as they are now, Jesus will surely protect them. Wally just wants his Wall St. job back. Wanda prays for revenge.

Somewhere in Wherever-The-Fuck, the mind of God is processing it all.

Its answer is, "Cuz that's just how it is."

X IS FOR XENOMORPHS

If there's one thing that could totally survive this, it's the alien from *Alien*.

TO THE AIR DUCT, YOU XENOMORPHIC SACK OF SHIT!

Y IS FOR "IT'S UP TO YOU"

Because it is.

Z IS FOR GROUND ZERO

Because that is where we live.

Intro to
THE INWARD EYE

This is by far the most autobiographical piece of fiction I've ever written.

I'll leave you to guess just how much of it is real.

THE INWARD EYE

Dear Professor Motherfucking Maynard Wills --

Wow! And WOOO-HOO-HOO!!! Thank you for your insanely synchronistic message of inquiry. I gotta admit, I haven't a clue as to how or why you plucked my name out of your mystery hat, given the gazillions of media freaks and conspiracy junkies out there to choose from. It's not like I've ever gone on the record with this shit.

But your timing couldn't be better, as the odds are 50/50 or worse that this may be my last goddam night on earth. And given the nature of the topic at hand, I guess that's just par for the course.

The universe works in mysterious ways.

And that ain't but the half of it.

As it turns out, yeah, I have plenty to say about your "Eyeless Man", although (as you'll see) I might describe him somewhat differently. Let's just say I know him well. And he knows me, a whole lot better than I wish he did. Never more so than now.

The bulk of the enclosed, as fate would have it, is a piece I've been working on for the last several weeks, in between wrapping my last remaining deadlines, locking down my last will and testament, making a point of telling all the people I love how much I love them, and fending off the itching in my brain with as much beer as I can swallow. Before the acid kicks in.

You wouldn't believe how hard it is to scratch the itch in your brain, once it gets started. Unless you already know. Which I pray that you don't.

Fingers can't reach it. There's a skull in the way.

But you do what you can. So I'm cutting and pasting the most pertinent bits in. As a researcher, I suspect that providing my case history might come in handy. At the very least, it provides context for the crazy-ass shit I'm about to say.

The question, of course, is: am I crazy? And the answer is, well, of course! Ask anyone! I've been weird since well before the day I was born, whether you measure that in embryonic terms, or pre-suppose (as I do) an endless litany of past lives, with an equally infinite litany of future lives to come.

This is what gives me hope, on my way through forever.

I hope to God, or whatever you wanna call it, that what I have to share is useful. And that it's not too late for you. Should you choose to publish it, I would think that was fucking great. But just in case, I'm cc'ing it to my family and most trusted friends. The last drip in my bucket list.

So STRAP IN, BABY! This is gonna take a while.

Here's hoping I make it all the way.

PART ONE: INTRODUCTION TO CONSCIOUSNESS. PRIMING MY RECEPTORS, AND THE ROAD TO HELL AND BACK

I'm not sure precisely when I first became aware of the vibrational frequencies underlying all existence. I'm guessing as ripples through my mother's amniotic fluid, as I gradually took form, moving from zygote to meatwad to flipper-sprouting eyeballed thing full of nerve endings on their way to babyness.

I don't know if you've read Stanislav Grof's brilliant *Beyond the Brain* (1985). But if you haven't, you probably should. It's without a doubt the smartest, most comprehensible book I've ever read about the actual nature and evolution of consciousness itself. (Grof's one of the founders of transpersonal psychotherapy, and a serious psychedelic researcher. A contemporary of Terrence McKenna, in the post-Leary years.) And it spends some serious time on the rigors of the pre-birth experience.

People tend to think of life beginning the second you pop out of the womb. But that's even dumber than thinking life begins or ends in high school. Fact is, we spend months taking shape before the nascent brain grows a single fissure. And yet we are -- albeit at the most basic level -- aware.

(And no, for the record: this is not a pro-life message. At that point, I was just another lump of meat struggling to be born, just like every other creature on this world or any other. *I made it! BALLOONS FOR ME!*)

But I know for a fact that my mother loved the music of Rosemary Clooney, and the laughter of studio audiences on radio talk and game shows. Not sure if TV existed in our home yet. (It was 1956 when I was "conceived".) My oldest sister was in love with rock 'n' roll. The sound of rebellion in that era. Elvis Presley in my DNA.

So it only makes sense that -- as I grew ears, and a brain at functional minimum, and a heart that could beat by itself -- I was receiving those signals. Not as loud as Mom's comforting heartbeat, which was huge. But they were already having their way with me.

Which means that advertisements were also sneaking in. With their own insidious vibrations.

More on that in a minute.

My earliest actual memory -- recounted in various interviews over the years, and most specifically in the novel *The Cleanup* -- is of the day the rats came down the walls.

I can't recall the specifics of my little boy bedroom. I can't tell you what was on the TV. (Which we had, at that point. It was 1960, and I was three-anna-half years old.) And I certainly didn't know that my experience was -- as far as my parents and sisters were concerned -- a hallucination.

All I knew was that the rats were pouring down the walls. Malformed. Spindle-legged. And sharp of teeth. Black pearl eyes glistening. As they chittered, descending.

They came like torrential rain, sluicing the walls to either side. Not dropping on me from the ceiling -- I have no memory of the ceiling -- but with an M.C. Escher-like pattern of infinite onslaught. Dozens unto hundreds of thousands. Not just pouring, put pooling underneath me. Like a maelstrom of hunger into which I would be swept.

And I remember screaming. Not just baby screams. Not "WAAAAH! My diaper is pooped!" Or "WAAAAH! You said no, and I don't like it!"

It was my first experience with genuine terror.

I remember my dad, scooping me up and yelling words I didn't understand. But I knew he was scared, too. Our frequencies conjoining.

Then I was in the bathtub, and my mom and dad were there, pouring ice cubes upon me as the chill water flowed. Burning off my fever. My delirium fever. As I screamed and screamed. Body engulfed in rising cold.

And this was the thing: *the second the rats hit the water, they vanished.* Not dissolving. Just ceasing to exist.

Then the fever broke, and they stopped coming.

It was a total *Jacob's Ladder* experience. And taught me, for the first time, the difference between my inner and outer experience.

Some might say it's about the difference between delirium and fact.

Me, I might beg to differ.

In the childhood years that followed, I took in everything the world shot my way. Fell in love with cartoons, which brought me joy and fun and chaos. Cartoons were where ANYTHING could happen, and usually did. Bugs Bunny and Daffy Duck ruled my world. Old Max and Dave Fleischer *Popeye* shorts. Those vibrations were not lost on me. Are my lifeline, to this day.

The news, back then, had a gray stentorian tone. The "Voice of Authority". It was male. It was old. Wore a stupid suit and tie. Shot in black and white, but totally white in presentation. (That said -- living in the West Allis suburb of Milwaukee, Wisconsin -- I'd never met anyone who *wasn't* white, so I had no broader frame of reference.)

My main impressions were that a) I didn't understand a thing they said, and b) I found no comfort there. If this was the wider world, I wasn't sure I liked it. It didn't feel good, that much was for sure. It made me want to leave the room, or beg them to turn back to cartoons.

But then -- one Saturday afternoon, somewhere between *The Flintstones*, *The Jetsons*, and *Top Cat* -- the terror frequency came back, in the form of a commercial for *Dr. Cadavarino's Late-Night Monster Movie Show*.

The monster in question was *Frankenstein*.

And, in my soul, the rats returned.

I didn't know who Boris Karloff was. But there was something in his flattened skull, his haunted eyes, his shambling gate that took me straight to panic. A bandwidth I knew all too well, and had all but forgotten, until that moment.

I shrieked and ran from the TV room to the dining room, howling desperately for my mom. The room was dim, the curtains pulled. And she was nowhere to be found.

When the footsteps started pounding up the creaking basement stairs, I hid under the table, quaking, until Mom dragged me out, consoled me, and informed me that monster movies were strictly off-limits.

But, of course, I had tasted the forbidden fruit.

The first scary movie I watched in its entirety -- alone, at the ripe old age of six -- was the 1953 science fiction classic *Invaders From Mars*. And, of course, it scared the living shit out of me. The notion that space creatures had landed in the field out back of this little kid's house, creating suckholes of cosmic quicksand that could drag you under, and send you back alien and transformed -- or, worse yet, *do that to your parents* -- was purest nightmare fuel. And left me seriously questioning authority for the very first time.

Underneath all that, though, was the music. Music designed specifically to induce fear and dread. Up until then, the creepiest music I'd ever heard was "Dance of the Sugar Plum Fairies", in Music Appreciation Class (a class they actually used to teach in elementary school). Which I loved. But this was something else.

It was, I believe, my introduction to the theremin: the first pre-Moog electronic instrument. Its unearthly portamento sweeps and hovering vibratos sent chills from my skull down to my toenails. I knew this was something that changed the frequencies of *my* world. And suspected this was true of the world at large.

At which point, I was hooked.

From there, I watched every horror movie I could get my eyeballs on. And quickly drew the distinction between the ones that were genuinely scary and the ones that were just laughably stupid. But those were beautiful, too. They put the terror in perspective, and allowed me to realize I didn't have to be scared. That they were, in their way, just as funny as cartoons.

And by the time The Beach Boys slapped a theremin on "Good Vibrations", as its signature feel-good sound, I felt pretty well integrated.

Then my family moved to Buenos Aires, Argentina, when my dad got a job with the State Department. And several life-altering things transpired.

1) I witnessed actual violence and death, mostly at the hands of an authoritarian regime where even the traffic cops carried machine guns. Saw people beaten to death in front of me. Saw rivers of blood flow down the steps of a *futbol* stadium, after a riot over a 0-0 match between rival teams River and Boca that I'd hoped to attend on my birthday, but mercifully missed. Thereby opening my deep well of sorrow.

Now I knew that death was real, because I could smell the blood and see the bullet holes. Horror wasn't just a fantasy. It was an actual fact. And it could happen to me, if I didn't watch my ass.

2) I discovered psychedelic music. First from purchasing my first-ever record album, *Sgt. Pepper's Lonely Hearts Club Band*, by my absolute favorite band, The Beatles. Between "For the Benefit of Mr. Kite", "Within You, Without You", and "A Day in the Life", my world was sonically transformed by vibrations the world itself admitted had never been heard before.

Then I made friends with a kid named Donald Hunt, whose older brother was sending care packages from Berkley, California, the heart of the hippie scene. Suddenly, I was deluged by Frank Zappa and the Mothers of Invention's "The Return of the Son of Monster Magnet", Grace Slick's witchy crooning on Jefferson Airplane's "White Rabbit" and "Lather", and -- most of all -- the unparalleled trippy delirium of Jimi Hendrix on guitar, ripping apart and recalibrating forever what six strings and a piece of wood could do.

3) This led to the purchase of my first electric guitar: a sunburst Stratocaster copy hanging in a music store window, which I demanded my parents purchase for me. So I could follow that path myself.

And here's the hilarious thing. They bought it for me. I had never been more excited in my life. We took it home. Plugged it into a stereo amplifier.

But because the amp was running on 120 volts of U.S. current, and the transformer adapting it ran on the Argentine 220...

...I was electrocuted, from the moment my fingers hit the strings. Frozen in place, as the maladapted voltage poured through me. Paralyzed. Juddering like jello on a spring. As the world went white and shuddery and gone.

In that moment -- for the first time -- I ceased to be myself. I was pure screaming energy. Mind erased. Body almost irrelevant.

My sister Reenie -- the only one in the room -- thought it was the funniest thing she ever saw, right up until she realized I might be truly dying. At which point, she had the smarts to pull the plug out of the wall.

A sane person might have called it quits right there. But again, I have never claimed to be sane.

So we got a new amp that wouldn't kill me. And I taught myself how to play, by ear. Mimicking every bass note, every chord change, every riff of the music that captivated me. Song by song. Lick by lick. Melody by melody.

I couldn't touch the sonics of Jimi or Frank or The Beatles. I had no fuzz box, no Wah-Wah pedal, no EchoPlex. But I understood that the music itself cast a spell, no matter what instrument you played it on. That songs told stories, carried direct experiences. And that music didn't need words to tell you how it felt, and make you feel it.

By the time I was forced to flee Argentina -- when the military overthrew President Ongania, and the tanks were in the streets (where some people I knew were about to disappear, only be found 30 years later, in mass graves containing countless thousands of others) -- I was ready to return to the U.S. of A. I wanted to be part of the counterculture that was brewing. I wanted to see the live bands weave their sonic magick onstage. I wanted to *be* in one of those bands, weaving magick of my own.

But almost most of all, I really wanted to do me some drugs.

I was 13 years old. It was 1970. And at Stratford Junior High School in Arlington, Virginia, drugs were everywhere. It didn't take long to find the cool kids at the smoking corner, who loved the same music, grew their hair long, wore the closest to hippie clothes their parents would let them get away with. And a lot of them were holding.

Over the next several years, I tried every mind-bending chemical known to teenage humankind. Quickly found I hated heroin. Hated speed. Hated downers. Was not super-fond of cocaine. Hated PCP (known as Angel Dust) with a passion: a drug so stupid that my body literally *forgot how to shit,* for several hours that seemed to last forever.

That said, I fell in love with weed, which has been my near-daily companion ever since. I consider it a benign and reliable entryway to fifth-dimensional experience. Attenuating my sensory apparatus. Colors sharper. Music deeper. That is my energetic comfort zone, and I ain't afraid to say it.

But the biggest game-changer was LSD, be it a sugar cube or a microdot or slip of blotter paper.

That was where my inner eye irrevocably opened at last.

Maynard, muh man? I really can't overstate the importance of psychedelic drugs, particularly as it pertains to your inquiry. Had I not dropped acid, I would never have had full waking access to the subconscious mind -- the stomping ground of dreams -- and the even deeper universal mind underlying all existence.

Cuz here's the thing. Peyote is great. If you want to talk with the Mushroom People from the Mushroom Dimension, right here on Earth, that's your big chance! They're out there (or in there, however you choose to frame it).

But LSD is the direct link between your central nervous system and the mind of God. All the doorways blown open. All the gates unlocked.

You wanna understand infinity as not just a concept, but a direct experience? Then I dare you to do what I used to do, on a regular basis, in those teenage years.

Drop some good clean acid, in a nice safe place. And as you start to hit the hallucinatory peak, FORCE YOURSELF TO KEEP YOUR EYES SHUT FOR THE NEXT TWO HOURS AT LEAST.

What unspools there -- in profound SenSurround -- is a relentless onslaught of fractal unfurlement, the likes of which computer imagery has barely cracked the code (though the Brit animator Cyriak comes

super-close). One electric glowing image after another, in replicating
patterns both evocatively abstract and stunningly specific.
   Shapes, yes. Shambling. Slithering. Soaring.
   But mostly faces. Faces within faces. Faces morphing and mutating
into and out of each other. So that something unspeakably beautiful
decays into monstrous nightmare, turns cartoonishly comic, flows into
ineffably gorgeous again.
   All coming at me. Closing in. And blowing through me.
   It was there that I saw that all things were truly One. That what
we call life is a sliver of a fragment of a dream of the All That Is, as It
envisions itself in every possible configuration. A perpetual motion ma-
chine, reinventing itself micro-second by even quicker micro-second.
The pushme-pullyou that keeps infinity running forever. Boundlessly,
inexhaustibly creative. As It explores all that It might be.
   It was there that I first saw your Eyeless Man, over and over and
over again. Wearing many faces, of various shapes. Some with teeth
like stilettos. Some with no teeth at all, mouths as empty as the sockets
of his eyes.
   The thing that conjoined them was that empty space where the gaze
had sucked back to nothingness. Peering into me, without seeing the
real me at all. It was an absence of love or recognition.
   But his hunger was very real.

I ain't gonna lie to you. That was terrifying shit. You think he's
scary in sobriety? TRY HIM ON FUCKING ACID. It was all I
could do not to open my eyes, escape from him into what passes
for consensual reality.

What made it possible was the fact that he was only one of the
endless forces underlying the deeper reality.

He represented the pit into which I could fall, if I let myself.
A truly bottomless pit, where every landing I hit was a trap door
opening up to an even deeper darkness. Plummeting further and

further from the last stitch of light remaining. Until I was as lost as he.

For me, the saving grace was how quickly he transmuted, if I did not submit. His doorway was potent. But his doorway was fleeting. And I did not have to take it.

There were other options. Like light, for instance. Like love. Like joy. He was just another color on the palette. With so many more to choose from, in the vast sprawl of life.

This became clear when I finally joined, then formed, my own bands, getting the tools at last with which to unleash my own vibrations. I had a '65 Strat, and all manner of gizmos to unleash with, playing guitar at least five hours a day, every day. I was writing my own songs, shaping my sadness and hope into sonic vision. And I can't tell you how many hours I spent noodling around on synthesizers, even though I couldn't play keyboards for shit: exploring the filters, plumbing the frequencies, experimenting with soundscapes at every range, down to the subsonic. Where I felt, rather than heard, what was blowing back at me.

All of this dramatically changed how I perceived all other media. Not just music, where I could smell the insincerity of most pedestrian pre-fab radio pop. Now every commercial ad psychically reeked of naked greed I could not help but taste on my mind's tongue, and wanted to spit out as fast as possible. Almost all network television left me feeling the same way.

Little wonder I became an outlaw, at least in my own mind.

All of which came into sharp, profound focus, when my past lives began to flash before me.

The first one hit in 9th Grade detention, where I was serving time for calling out a bullying math teacher on his abuse of one of the slower kids. ("Excuse me, Mr. Miller," I said. "I know it's easy to pick on poor ol' Butch. But how'd you like to try that shit on me?")

So there I was, doodling weird faces and shapes cartoonily into my notebook, while the principal called my mom…

…*and suddenly, I was on fire, tied to a stake in front of a leering crowd. I could smell my hair burn to either side of my face, as the flames licked up. Smell my own meat crackling. Could feel the off-the-charts pain blaze through me*…

…*and in that moment, I knew I was a young woman, unjustly accused of being a witch*…

…*and I was soooooooo angry at being killed for this*…

…and then the bell rang, dragging me back to the classroom. Where I sat, drenched in sweat. Wondering what the hell just happened to me.

But it wasn't the last time.

Over the next many years, I found myself spontaneously flashing back to other lives. A young Native pre-American brave, taking an arrow through the throat from a rival tribe, falling back into a stream where I drowned as I bled out. Others too muzzy for me to recollect, but sooooo vivid as they happened. Leaving marks upon my soul. Or perhaps just alerting me to the marks already there.

Were they past lives? Was it genetic memory, my DNA randomly squirting out its encoded history? Or was I just hallucinating, my brain playing tricks based on some kind of faulty wiring?

I had no way of knowing. My entire way of knowing had been thrown into question.

All I could say was that it felt real to me. Every bit as real as everything else.

So when I suddenly found myself getting glimpses of Heaven, the only frame of reference I had was my own experience.

That's when shit really started to get weird.

Suddenly, I was an angel. I knew that for a fact. I had ascended as far as I could go, as a soul. Was experiencing unparalleled beauty and peace. The true fulfillment of all that I might be.

And yet, as I gazed down on all creation, I saw unspeakable suffering and torment. Staggering injustice. Wrong after wrong after wrong. Saw the terrestrial food chain tear itself apart, and swallow itself, through every mouth ever opened. Felt the pain of every tooth and claw.

So I said to God, "What the fuck is this? I mean, here we are in perfection. You can clearly do anything. You can clearly do everything! So why is this allowed to happen?"

And God said, "That's just the way it is."

Needless to say, I was not satisfied with this answer. And I was not the only one. There were a bunch of angels who were right there with me. Including this guy named Lucifer -- aka The Light-Bringer *-- who was the most beautiful and radiant one of all. Going, "Dude, this is totally not cool. We think you need to change this. Like, starting right now."*

But God said, "No."

Just like that, there was war in Heaven. A small army of us, rising up, in an attempt to force the issue.

Unfortunately for us, God's faithful were stronger; and under the leadership of Generalissimo Archangel Michael, we thoroughly got our asses kicked in short order.

At which point, we were vanquished to Hell. Where we languished for the next untold-trillion years, if time existed at all.

But while the newly-renamed Lucifer (now Satan, or The Adversary) has been widely quoted as saying, "Better to rule in Hell than serve in Heaven", my personal experience was vastly different. For one thing, I wasn't ruling.

For another, they didn't call Hell "Hell" for nothin'.

It was the worst fucking place in God's creation. Specifically created by God, in order to house and punish all the worst of the worst in one place. Deploying the deepest cruelty, the most punishing punishment, upon many of the biggest assholes ever unleashed on said creation, from any and every domain.

I'm not saying there weren't some really good parties. If there's one thing I can tell you, it's that evil knows how to party. And some might argue that truly horrible sex is better than no sex at all. (I am not one of them.)

What I mostly felt was a bottomless sorrow, a smothering sense of loss. To have been wrenched from such heights, and thrown all the way down to this sulphurous soul-pit of ultimate degradation, was the authentic God-damned definition of unbearable for me.

I had no aptitude or inclination toward torturing others. It was the last thing I'd ever have wanted to do. Making me complicit in the very thing I'd fought against was the worst punishment I could possibly have imagined.

Was I furious? Absolutely. Did I feel like I'd been wronged? Without a doubt. Did I blame myself? I wasn't sure. I still thought that we were right

But did I hate myself, for having screwed up so royally?

Oh, baby, more than you will ever know.

All I really knew was that I refused to be this fallen angel. This was not what I wanted. This was not who I am.

And even if it took for-fucking-ever, I had to get out of this place.

I don't know how I managed to escape. All I know is that I did. My eyes on the beacon at the heart of All-That-Is.

And so -- for life after life after life -- I gradually crawled my way back to and through the land of the living. Step by step. Incarnation by incarnation. Learning the lessons that might take me back to the place where I hoped I belonged.

Now, Professor, just to be clear: I'm not saying that all this personal vision represents any kind of certifiable fact. I mean, I'm not even a fucking Christian. But I went to some Catholic schools, read enough of the Bible to get the gist. So that whole mythic template was yet another set of symbols and wavelengths I'd attempted to integrate, on the infinite road to understanding.

All I can say is, those were the flashes that came to me unbidden. Sometimes tripping. Sometimes just walking down the street, or laying in bed, or taking a leak.

And all of this has informed my perspective, all along this strange path.

Which brings us, at last, to the heart of your inquiry.

PART TWO: THE WHITE TAPE, AND ME

Flash-forward almost twenty years. My musical career never panned out, but I wound up on the New York Times bestseller list, writing outsider horror fiction that attempted to translate those trippy frequencies, nightmares, and gnostic longings into prose.

Suddenly, I was semi-famous. The only kind of rock star I would ever be. Millions of people had bought my work, whether they liked it or not. And a lot of them did. For better or worse, they were surfing my wave.

This resulted in fan mail. And in the pre-internet days, this came either through forwards from my publisher or people who tracked me down sideways. My listing in the phone book. A friend of a friend of a friend.

It was the era of VHS. And I was now devouring movies as hard as I'd once devoured albums, or novels. Had hundreds in my collection. Some bought. Most taped off cable.

But every once in a while, somebody would send me a tape of rarified shit I was not liable to find in my local video store, or pretty much anywhere else.

There were three of particular note.

The first was autopsy footage of a drowning victim, from a local York County, PA coroner's office. She didn't look like a person anymore. She had been bloated and rubberized by death into something that more resembled a shabby special effect from a C-grade monster movie. At first, that's what I thought it was.

But the more they methodically peeled her apart, the clearer it became that this was all real.

"Thought you'd like this!" said the coroner fan.

I didn't. It hurt. Took me down the dark hole. I could smell the formaldehyde rot, and deeply felt the indignity of this poor person, organ-splayed step-by-step before me. It was not something that was meant for me to see.

But it was real, and it was true. And I watched it all the way through. Did not feel like the person who sent it meant me harm. They just wanted me to know, in case I didn't.

I kept that tape in my collection for many years. Though I never watched it again.

The next (unlabeled, with no return address) was a compilation of bestiality scenes: women getting fucked by dogs, or sticking snakes up their vaginas. All shot on video, in trailer parks or shabby hotels. The women all tragically hot young junkies who rolled their eyes, not even bothering to fake it. Radiating narcotized despair, and the hope beyond hopelessness that this next fix might somehow help wipe their memory clean.

I watched as much as I could stand. Then took the tape out back and beat it to death with a hammer, shredding the loops of tape that unspooled so that nobody else would ever have to suffer that shit on my account. Tossing it all in the trash, as I shook off the heartbreaking vibrations as best I could. Which took a while.

And then came the White Tape. Unlabeled as well, like the last one. No name on the return address (which turned out to be false). Just the initials I.C.U.

But on the white VHS was a Post-It in the center, with the words "YOU WANT TO KNOW WHAT REAL HORROR IS?" in a jagged scrawl that looked like they could barely keep the pen from shaking out of their hand.

That was my first warning sign. And after the last two surprise tapes, I was a little gun-shy, to say the fucking least.

So I took the tape upstairs with me to my office, as I set into my day and night of writing. And only after my daughters and sweetheart were in bed and fast asleep did I venture back down to the living room. Grab a Rolling Rock from the kitchen. Fire up a bowl. And pop the tape in the VCR, then settle back on my couch to see what they claimed real horror was.

I will never forget the moment I picked up the remote and hit play.

It wasn't the image on the screen. I don't even remember the image on the screen. Have no idea whether I ever saw it or not.

It was the sound that hit me. More precisely, the sound beneath the sound. A susurrating roar of wrongness that vibrated in my bone marrow, forced the sweat from my pores in rivers.

The feeling was so intense, so instantaneous, that it felt like an acid flashback made of daggers. Stabbing every nerve ending I had with live wires, like the long-ago electric guitar that electrocuted me.

Once again, I left my body. But this time, the world was not shimmering white.

This time, all was black. A shimmering blacker-than-black.

And the Eyeless Man was there. No other faces. Only his.

"You think you know," he said, through a cavernous grin that threatened to swallow his features entirely. "You think you remember. You want to dance with the angels again. But there are no angels here."

It was true. In this black, crackling space, there was no room for light, nor appetite for it. He didn't give a shit about my light.

It was my darkness he craved.

As he pulled me toward him.

"Come in," he said, black sockets blazing with the anti-heat of a trillion nullified suns. "Let me remind you how I see."

The next thing I knew, I was inside his skull, crawling up inside his brain. The fissures like rows upon rows of occupied seats in a coliseum so huge my own skull threatened to crack at the enormity.

And every seat was taken by a glowing eye, staring down on me.

That was when I learned he was not eyeless at all.

They were all on the inside. Aimed directly at me.

Calling me back to Hell.

I can only guess that it was my body, working in self-defense, that made my thumb hit the stop button on the remote. Dragged me back to my seat on the living room couch. As I crapped my pants, and vomited onto the coffee table, my beer, my bowl of weed.

Like I couldn't get him out of me fast enough.

But, of course, it was too late.

PART THREE: WHERE IT GOES FROM HERE

It's been nearly thirty years since the events of that night. I'm 62 years old, as of this writing. Quite possibly the last writing that I will ever do. But we shall see.

I gotta admit, these last years have been largely great. I'm grateful to have lived this long, learned this many lessons. Wouldn't mind sticking around a while longer. I dearly love life. Have dearly loved this life, in particular, which I feel has brought me closer back to Godhead than I've been in a billion trillion years.

What I learned was that I would have to lean into life and love harder, even as the darkness assailed me. Try as you might, you can't beat up evil, or sweet-talk it into not being what it is. Played on its own terms, resistance is futile.

All you can do is try to be a better person. Help others whenever you can. Shine light on the darkness. Showing it what for what it is. Because it's never gonna go away. Nor should it. It is part of the design. An intrinsic and important part.

But that doesn't mean you fucking let it win.

Once I peeled off my shit-caked pants, put on new ones, and cleaned the puke off the table, I was left with the question of the White Tape, still sitting in my VCR. I didn't even want to touch it. The thought occurred to be: *should I just take the whole machine out? Maybe the shelf it sat on? Does the TV need to go? SHOULD I JUST BURN THE WHOLE HOUSE DOWN?*

Eventually, I grabbed an oven mitt and a can of lighter fluid. Popped the eject button. Grabbed the tape with the mitt, as it slid out. Took it out past the back alley, into the field behind my house. Kicked a pre-existing hole in the dirt to make it deeper. Dropped the tape and the mitt. Doused them profusely. And burned it all to molten sludge.

Then I got a bag of rock salt from the tool shed. Poured it over the sludge, and melted it, too.

Then I covered it with dirt, and salted the goddamned earth five feet in every direction. So that nothing might ever grow there again.

Then, just to be safe, I tossed the VCR in the trash, and bought a new one the next day.

As fate would have it, my TV was not possessed, and the walls of the house were not infected with the horror. My kids were fine. My lady was fine. We watched cartoons and scary movies, threw parties, loved each other, and lived life there quite nicely through all the ups and downs for a couple more years, before moving to California.

The only one infected was me.

And the good news is, I guess, that it took this long to catch up with me. That I toughed it out this far, even as I've watched that dark vibration spread further and further into the mediascape. Yes, in ugly movies and music. Yes, in ugly TV. Yes, in advertisements. Yes, especially, in the news.

But mostly in social media, where the Eyeless Man is everywhere projecting its solipsistic inward gaze, then squirting it out, one trillion rage-Tweets at a time, through every hapless soul who ever sucked the venom. Even at low doses, that shit adds up.

You might think I'm totally nuts, at this point, and you're certainly right. Who wouldn't be? And more to the point, WHO ISN'T? All things being equal, I sincerely doubt I'm the craziest sonofabitch you reached out to. Especially if they watched the White Tape.

In terms of evidence trail, though:

A couple weeks back, I had some brain scans done, because the itching inside my skull had finally become intolerable. And what they showed was not some big tumor, but *hundreds of tiny little nodes*, draped in every cranial crevice like pebbles. Too small to see the almost infinitesimally irises and pupils that I know for a fact they contain.

I got the results tonight, half an hour before I got your email.

Now it's an hour-anna-half later. And though my very last hit of acid is kicking in hard, I've tried at least that hard to stay focused, so that I might share this with you. In the hope, as I said, that it's helpful. Because we need all the help we can get.

All I ask is that you share what I've just shared with you, unexpurgated. Cuz it's the best I've got.

In a couple minutes, I'm going into the garage. My housemate Darren is a carpenter. He saws boards for a living. Is constructing a really sweet backyard awning, so we can sit on that porch in the Portland rain without getting drenched, as we party together. That's a thing I would dearly love to do.

But I always said that I would save my last LSD trip for my death bed. Part going-away present. Part welcome-back present. Welcoming myself back to the All-That-Is.

Turns out there is no bed in there. But there is a big-ass table, with a big-ass power saw I've strategically placed at the end. Right where my forehead goes.

I also brought out a couple of synthesizers, pre-programmed to spin out my favorite frequencies. And an amp wired to some super-sweet effects pedals, so I can play my Fender Stratocaster to my heart's content, as I lay down.

In a couple minutes, I will play my heart and soul out, as I close my eyes, and let infinity unleash upon me once again. The sweet and the sorrowful. The benign and malign. The comic and tragic. The pain and the gain.

And we shall see what we shall see.

If God tells me I'm not done, I will stick around as long as I can. As I was told long ago, and now finally get: *that's just the way it is.*

But if God agrees that I have ridden this particular roller coaster as far as it goes, then I will bring that whirling blade down on my forehead, hard. Sawing all the way through.

Cuz if that motherfucker doesn't scratch the itch, I frankly do not know what will.

My hope is that the light shines bright. As I dive into the infinite. Not for the last time. For the next.

But the fact is that the rats are back. Streaming down the walls. Pooling at my feet. And this time, they're biting. Wrenching psychic meat from cosmic bone, while the not-so-Eyeless Man presides.

They want me back. But I ain't going.

My own inner eye is clear.

Intro to
LITTLE DEUCE

Not too long ago, I was kindly invited to address a large group of 6th graders on Zoom, as part of a writing class. With a focus on "how to nail the ending." Which is a thing I think about all the time.

But when the teacher asked me if I had a piece of age-appropriate fiction I could share with the class, before we talked, I said, "Actually, no. Not even close. But if you give a minute, I'll write one for you!"

The result is, without a doubt, the only thing in this book with no swear words in it. Which clearly marks it as the only story with a speck of decency that I have ever done.

But, from what I gather, they liked it anyway! And the class was fantastic.

LITTLE DEUCE

I wake up on the floor in the new cave, stalactites jutting down from the roof like teeth. There's a cool breeze from the center of the earth, and I snuggle my blankets around me, warm and close. Thinking oh, *this is beautiful. I hope we get to stay.*

I can hear Mama by the fire pit, the sound of crackling wood, the smell of woodchuck and taters freshly pulled up by their roots. I love a good groundhog stew in the morning. It gets me out of my covers, ready to start my big day.

"Good morning, honey!" she calls to me as I stagger into the main chamber, still loopy from sleep. I give her a hug, and she squeezes me back with her free hand, still stirring the cauldron with the other. "Your clothes are hanging out front, okay? I washed 'em in the creek, but they should be dry in half an hour."

"Hope so!" I say, squinting at the sunlight blazing through the cave's entrance. Slip on my sunglasses, and wander out into the glowing world.

The water in the creek is icy cold as I bathe, nightgown resting on a rock by the shore. My wild tresses whip around my face, dripping and delighted. No fish come near. No animals. Just the trees, looming sightless overhead. The distant sun. And me.

By the time I get back, my clothes are almost dry, hanging from the low branches of the great oak by the hole in the mountain where we live. I dress, go inside. The stew is ready. I gulp it down like the starving girl I am.

"I hope they'll be nice this time," I say. Hoping against hope.

"Just be careful, Little Deuce" she says. "I love you."

"I will," I say. "I love you, too."

"And if you have to…" She pauses. "Just do what you gotta do."

There is no school bus that goes to the middle of the woods. So I walk the two miles alone till I hit the outskirts of town, walk the thirty more blocks to the parking lot of Jefferson Davis Junior High.

I pause there for a moment, see the hundreds of students milling out front. See the cliques: smart kids, jock kids, popular, pretty, unpopular, not so pretty. Fat. Skinny. Funny. Scared. Shy or aloof. Same as every school.

But none of them look like me.

I wrap the shawl tighter around my wild tresses, pull my sunglasses tighter to my burning eyes.

Am I scared? Yes, I am. Am I excited? Yes, that, too. This is my first middle school, after a couple dozen elementaries, moving from town to town to town.

I wait until the bell rings, and the crowd all moves inside, before heading for the front door.

But, of course, the last stragglers are the mean ones. And the second they see me, they zero in. Staring at me as one. Grinning. Leering. Elbowing each other.

"Oh, lookie here!" says Junior Varsity Bob, oversized teeth gleaming in his zit-pocked face.

"What is THAT?" quips Cheerleader Sue. "Is that a Martian? Or is she from the Middle East?"

"This ain't no Middle Eastern school!" laughs Titanic Todd, the barely-teenage man mountain standing six foot two. "It's just a middle school. But maybe you don't know that, cuz you can't read English."

And everyone laughs. But I keep walking forward.

"I speak English," I say. "Probably better than you."

"OOOO!" says the mob in unison, closing in on me. Like that's supposed to scare or shame me.

"I just want to go to class," I say. "So if you'll please excuse me…"

"Well, maybe we don't want you in our class," says Todd, the others gathered around him. Blocking me. Surrounding me in a half-ring. "Maybe we don't want you here at all."

And that's when I know this is not going to work out. The door is ten yards away. I bet I'll never make it in.

Still, I keep my hands at my sides. I will not be the one to start this.

I wait until they get right up in my face, throwing swear words and insults and mocking laughter.

I wait until Cheerleader Sue swats the sunglasses off my blazing eyes.

Then I stare at them, as they freeze in place.

I pull off my shawl, releasing the writhing snakes beneath it. All staring as well.

I watch their skin turn gray as granite rock, features locked in sudden terror. Watch their eyes turn to gleaming beads of stone. Then watch the gleaming fade to blank.

I wonder if the parents of these jerks will put the statues that remain of them in their yards. Or make them their gravestones.

Right this second, I really do not care.

Then I walk the two miles and change back to our cave.

And say, "Mama Medusa? I think we're gonna need another school."

Intro to
THE SHITTIEST GUY IN THE WORLD:
A CHRISTMAS FABLE

Don't get me wrong. I looooove Christmas. Whether you view it as a celebration of God's miraculous plan for our salvation, a cultural appropriation, or a cynical cash grab, I've got nothing bad to say about a ritual where we give each other presents, to make each other happy, because we love each other. Wish we could do it every day.

That said -- and a warning to the wise -- if you ask me to write a fucking Christmas story, it'll probably wind up something like this.

THE SHITTIEST GUY IN THE WORLD (A CHRISTMAS FABLE)

The shittiest guy in the world is curled up in his bed on Christmas Eve, plump and rosy in his satin pajamas. He's an investment banker whose specialty is toxic mortgages, so it's a very, very nice bed.

In fact, pretty much everything on his 30-acre gated Malibu estate is nice but him. His swimming pool. His tennis court. His Hummer H1, his Tesla, his Porsche, the other seventeen sets of wheels in his collection. The private movie theater in which he screens the Adam Sandler and Michel Bay flicks that make him an extra couple mil per year on the side whether anybody goes to see them or not is state-of-the-art. Because he can afford it. He can afford almost anything.

He likes owning nice things. As many as possible. And doing whatever he wants to them, whenever the fuck he wants. Far as he's concerned, he owns everyone and everything. They just don't know it yet.

The stunningly-exquisite submissive high-end escort he just spent the last three hours abusing and tormenting was substantially – substantially – nicer than him. "Merry Christmas, whore!" were his parting words. He tipped her a ten-dollar bill, which he tossed on the marble floor, so she had to stoop to retrieve it before heading home to her very nice daughter and entire reason for living.

Like I said: the shittiest guy in the world.

And there he is: sleeping like a baby, snoring like a moose, ripped on coke and thousand-year-old cognac. Far as he's concerned, he's the king of the world. Ain't nothin' gonna touch this guy.

He doesn't see the creeping shadows glide across the Picassos that adorn his walls. Doesn't see the pint-sized shapes who cast them, creeping ever closer. His expensive alarm system is entirely untriggered. His security crew – all brutal goons, but still a trillion times nicer than him – goes entirely unalerted.

It isn't until they jump onto the bed that he stirs in dull, semi-comatose surprise.

But when the first one kneels down and punches him right in the kisser, that definitely gets his attention. He goes "YAUGH!", sinks into the pillows on impact, three teeth dislodged and aimed straight down his airhole.

His bleary eyes flicker open, see a bright pointy cap on the top of a small whiskered shadow. Another beside it. One red-capped. One green. Both with eyes that blaze rage in the darkness.

The second one stomps on his copious gut, and the shittiest guy in the world sits up: blinded with pain, whooping for air, teeth draped in a thin red halitosis spray as they sail onto his lap.

He doesn't see the bright green sack being swooped over his head until it's already smothering him, pulling down and down, rough hands lifting his ass up the way he removed the escort's panties, then pulling it all the way to his feet and beyond. Until he's entirely encased. With a knot at the end.

Next thing he knows, he's being dragged off the bed, falling, hitting the marble hard. Then he's dragged across the room, into the hall, and down the stairs, one pummeling thump-thump-thump after another. Squealing and bellowing, to no avail.

Through the fabric of the bag, he can see the bright lights of his enormous Christmas tree come into muted view. A twenty-footer, every inch of it coated in pure gold flake and festooned with $10.5 million in shimmering bling. He does a new one every year. It is his Christmas tradition.

When they come to the fireplace, he instantly regrets having lit up a fire inside it. It cast great shadows on the whore's ass as he flailed and nailed it, yes. But now the flames are down to coals.

They flare for a second, as he is tossed in upon them. Screaming. And then up the flume he goes.

Five whooshing seconds later, he lands like a sack of meat on the rooftop. A couple seconds later, he hears thuds to either side. The animal whinny of a species he doesn't recognize is directly ahead. He is dragged toward it. Can smell the matted fur.

He hears the moaning of others, then: growing closer, muted as his own. He feels himself lifted, hoisted up by strong angry hands. Then dropped onto something that wriggles beneath him.

Twenty seconds later, they begin to fly.

From there, it's all fierce freezing wind and vertiginous momentum that seems to last forever. He can barely hear the moans of the dozens that surround him, all encased in their own festive kidnap bags.

He is numb long before the chill grows authentically arctic. And at last, they land.

The shittiest guy in the world is one of the first yanked off of the back, slammed to the ground, and dragged through the clanking dungeon door to an ugly dim-lit stone enclosure, where the stink of despair is only slightly more vibrant than the nonstop ululations of the damned.

It isn't until he hears the chink of steel gates opening then closing behind him that he is able to, at last, pull the bag off his head.

He is in an enormous medieval prison. There are easily a thousand others there that he can see. Every single one of them as terrified as he is. Every single one unable to comprehend how they could have possibly come to be in such a terrible place.

"What the fuck did I do? DON'T YOU KNOW WHO I AM?" howls one captive after another. No one louder than the shittiest guy in the world.

That's when a distant metal door clinks open, and a dowdy, adorable little old lady comes down the corridor, sporting a Christmasy apron and dress. She is flanked by a security force of short, pointy-hatted, fierce-eyed elves. Two of whom he thinks he recognizes.

"That one," she says, pointing, working her way down the aisle. "We do love our uncaught serial killers. Oh, and that one might turn out nice. I like his Saudi corporate oil deals, his pay-for-terrorists and exploit-all-women spice."

When she gets to the shittiest guy in the world, though, her grandmotherly eyes fire up. Nailing him like spotlights.

"Oh, but THIS little fellow!" she laughs out loud.

And that is the seal of approval.

Next thing he knows, he is being dragged out of the cell and harshly propelled down the corridor, past thousands and thousands more. Until he comes to the mouth of the grim gray stairwell, is poked and prodded up, up, up, away from the increasingly-echoing howls of despair.

And toward the mounting sound of warm and boisterous laughter.

And, oh, the smells that beckon from above...

The door at the top of the stairs opens into a vast, expansive and utterly charming old-fashioned fairy tale kitchen. The kind of kitchen dreams are made of, expanded unto near-infinity. Divinely lit. Both humbly quaint and frankly magnificent.

Hundreds of glimmering pots hang in rows on ceiling racks that go back and back to the vanishing point. Burnished wooden cabinets as far as the eye can see. Ovens the size of morgue vaults line the walls, one after another. So many stove tops a-simmer that it boggles the mind, all decanting olfactory delight.

And the smells are breathtaking. They are the smells of sweetest heaven.

The shittiest guy in the world goes "Whoa." Taking it all in. Instantly desirous. Calculating how much it would cost to own this, too. Already negotiating the deal in his head.

There is a long long long prep table as the kitchen's centerpiece. Fifty feet? A hundred feet? A million feet? Who knows? Like the kitchen, it stretches out beyond beyondness.

"Hey!" he says. "Who's in charge here? I think we can work this...AWKKK!"

Abruptly, he is hustled forward and lifted aloft like a deli tray, back and skull slamming down on the tabletop so hard he barely remembers who he is until the little old lady is hovering above him. Butcher knife in hand.

He starts to scream, and someone shoves an apple in his mouth. It catches in his teeth, stays there like a ball gag.

Elf hands peel off his satin pajamas, lift his ass up, leave him naked on display. There are at least a dozen elves holding him down, stripping him down, or standing back with razors at the ready in their hands.

Once every hair on his body has been shaved, the adorable little old lady guts his ass from dick to Adam's apple, methodically pulling out every unappetizing organ as she goes. Cancer-riddled intestines. Atrophied heart. While he screams and screams and screams.

They then anoint him with a rich honey glaze, add some zesty secret spices, and toss him in the oven for what seems like a million years.

He is awake and alive for every micro-second of searing pain. And every speck of it is monumental. Like burning in hell. Forever and ever.

Only then does the oven door open, and he finds himself slapped back on the table. Carved to the bone. And carried out on a platter, in slices and hanks, to the source of the warmth and laughter.

His head is intact. And his eyes, though baked, can blearily see the immense banquet table upon which he has been placed. It is lined with hungry, cheerful elves, clinking their goblets to either side.

At the head is the adorable old woman and her equally adorable, cherubic husband. With his classic red suit, and immense white beard. Chuckling with delight at the feast to come.

"Let us pray," Santa says. And all the rest bow their heads.

"Every year, on this day," he continues, "we nurture the spirit of giving. Giving is what we do. It's a beautiful thing."

Applause, around the table.

"But there is no bounty without balance. No reward without sacrifice. No gift without a price."

The shittiest man in the world desperately tries to name his price. But he can't. There's an apple ball-gagging his mouth. He has no guts left, and not a limb to stand on. He is sliced meat on a table.

The most ignominious end of all.

"So tonight, once again," Santa says, "we eat the sins of the very worst among us. Take their unjustness, their profound self-centeredness, their endless and arbitrary abuse of power, and transmute it to good. Take it into ourselves. And spread just a little bit of it to every struggling person on Earth who could use a little pure love tonight."

The glasses clink, in support of pure love.

And then they dig in, one dripping slice at a time. He is awake for every screaming bite. Until the last one. Then over and out.

But somewhere in North Hollywood, the lovely daughter of a very nice high-priced escort who has repeatedly eaten all the sins of the world – one ruthless man at a time – gets a hug, and a couple more presents than she might have otherwise dared hope for.

Along with everyone else he ever screwed. Everywhere. All over the world. Making their lives just a little bit better. Not remotely fair, but every little bit helps.

Christmas. Yes, it's a dirty job.

But somebody's gotta do it.

Intro to
NO MORPHIC FIELD LIKE HOME

Nothing breaks my heart like the toll this pandemic has taken on our sacred watering holes. Not just the devastating economic cost, but the loss of a never-all-that-safe space to let our hair down, dance and drink and maybe even hook up for the night.

This piece was inspired by my musical soundscape "Ghosts of Dive Bars Past", and the work of Rupert Sheldrake. A tragic love song of friendship, with a smile as its umbrella.

NO MORPHIC FIELD LIKE HOME

Tawny, Trayvon, and Candy were all the way gone, so Jane fixed herself a drink behind the bar. It was her bar, after all.

The power was still on, so there was plenty of ice. The glasses were dusty, so she rinsed hers off, wiped down the bottle of Tanqueray, spritzed tonic and gin on a couple of clinkety cubes. She had brought her own fresh lime, and carved a slice, which she squeezed over the glass like a sacrificial virgin in a dragon's jaws.

"Nooooo!" screamed the lime, in her cartooniest voice. "What did I ever do to yooooou?"

"You were delicious," she answered herself. "Your guts are the best."

"Gaaaagh!" The lime expired in a death rattle squirt. The only sound from the room.

Outside, there was nothing but wailing wind.

It had been ten months since the lockdown, the shutdown, the incident, and the barring of the doors. Ten months out of commission. On an ordinary Thursday night like tonight -- at Calamity Jane's, at closing time -- there would have been a dozen drunkasses or more, not counting the closing band. Fridays and Saturdays were better. Sunday broke about even. Monday through Wednesday were a wash. A rough business, on the best of days.

She missed her badass best friend Tawny, that raven hair and spitfire grin. Missed Jasper and Jonesy, their racist jokes (one white, one black), cheerfully poking holes in each other's cliches. Missed

Murphy the sound man, forever complaining but eternally on his game, no matter what prima donna was heading for the mic.

But now there was nothing but the empty stage in the empty room full of empty seats, as she tipped her glass to no one.

There was a gun next to the knife that gutted the lime. She didn't wanna go there yet.

"I love you," she said, to everyone and no one in particular. To the sense of community she'd loved and lost. Stolen by Covid. By economic collapse. By human frailty, doing what human frailty does. And, finally, by unspeakable violence.

"I miss you," she whispered.

And that was when Tawny floated through the bolted door.

It wasn't hard to walk through the door without a body. Way easier than losing that body had been. A bullet through the brainpan was nothing to sneeze at.

But based on Jane's sudden, startled smile, she didn't look like she did when her skull came apart.

"Hi, Janie!" she said, as Jane let out a whoop.

"OMIGOD!" Rattling the ceiling with joy.

"Are we really the only ones here?" Tawny let out a what-the-fuck gesture. "That don't seem right!"

"Oh, Tawny." Laugh-crying. "There ain't none of this right. But…"

"Yeah, I know," Tawny said. "But are you gonna come over here and hug me or what?"

Jane came around the bar so fast space and time were a blur, with an open-armed hug to unleash. So she shouldn't have been surprised when she blew right through her friend like a wisp of cigarette smoke, and screeched to a halt.

But Tawny was laughing behind her, and still there when she turned.

"Let's try that a little bit slower."

"Okay…"

She sidled up to her spectral friend, and embraced the space where the shape still held. She couldn't feel the arms that wrapped her back, or the body she pressed against.

But within that space, they were warm together. And that was something they could both feel, and bask in. Both laughing and weeping, as well.

"I'm not a ghost," Tawny said. "I'm not a haunted soul, doomed to wander the earth forever. I'm just a spirit. My spirit. And I wanted to say hi."

"Me, too!" yelled a voice from behind her, inside a cacophony of raucous laughs. A dozen, easy.

They weren't just coming through the door. They were coming through the windows and walls. Jake the Quake, from the band Funhammer, literally descending from the fucking ceiling. Always one for a grand entrance.

Suddenly, the room was flooded with grinning souls. A bit on the ethereal side, to be fair. But there. And clearly happy to be so. Hugging each other in flares of connection, then repeating the process around the length of the dive bar till everybody got a piece.

"WHO NEEDS A DRINK?" bellowed Trayvon, back behind the bar. And everyone yelled, "ME!"

Which was how it ought to be.

The night of the incident, things had not been so grand. Everybody tense. Even the best friends afraid of what might happen next. The election was coming. And there was no way it was gonna be pretty.

Calamity Jane's was a redneck bar, yes. Which meant working class. But that did not begin to nail them. Some leaned red. Some leaned blue. Some were anarchists. Some libertarians. Some apolitical, just there to have fun, didn't care to discuss or give a shit either way. They were not a cultural monolith.

It wasn't until the three rando Proud Boys blew into the parking lot at about 12:45 ayem, honking and waving their flags and yelling, "FUCK your feelings, LIBTARDS!" that the powder keg ignited.

The scrawny skinhead with the prison neck tattoos had a hard time parking his pickup truck, cuz he was clearly methed out of his skull. Jane was there to bear witness, grabbing a quick smoke by the front door with Tawny and Riley, their new head cook.

"Aw, shit," said Tawny. She was a survivalist, living out of her van and wherever she pitched her tent. Her danger radar was keen.

"I don't think those boys need another drink," Jane said. She'd been dealing with assholes her whole life. But this was putting a prickle on her skin as well.

It wasn't until they stumbled out with their AR-15s strapped on that she went into full alert.

"Oh, whoa whoa whoa," said Jane, stepping up and toward them. "You can't bring that shit in here."

"It's an open carry state, bitch," spat the 6 foot 6, 280-pound mountain of muscle closing in on her first.

"Yeah, that may be. But it's not an open carry bar. You can't fucking come in here with that shit."

"Says who?" said the beardo circling in from the driver's side, a couple steps behind him.

"Says me. It's my fucking bar."

"Well, then maybe you should shut the fuck up, and get out of our way. Before someone gets hurt."

It occurred to her that calling the cops might be a good idea. It also occurred to her that they were about six seconds away from blowing past her, through the door. She found herself backing up, found herself enraged. Looked behind her for Tawny and Riley. But they were already gone.

She didn't want her phone slapped out of her hand and broken. She didn't want her face punched in, or her head blown off. So she backed to the door, threw it open behind her. Stepped in. And pressed her feet against the other side, tugging back on the door handle with all her might.

The band was on break, so the jukebox was playing. Johnny Cash. "The Man in Black." And it seemed so perfect, in those final moments. Such a statement of hope, for the flawed human race.

But then the door yanked forward, and she bellowed "HELP!" as her sneakered heels skidded forward like careening wheels when the brakes were locked, and the crash was imminent.

The rest happened so fast she was barely able to clock it. She was skidding, then she was falling, the meaty fist to her temple sending her reeling to the floor. She felt the bodies move past her, heard the yelling in a muffled blur.

Next thing she knew, friends were rising from their seats: some surging forward, some holding others back, some beelining fast as they could toward the back exit. Everybody yelling, drowning out even Johnny Cash. At this moment, the only reasonable voice in the room.

Then the big guy who'd hit her started punching the fuck out of Jonesey, the first one to get in his face. Jaspar broke his longneck Blue

Moon bottle on the nearest table, brandished the jagged edges. Beardo pivoted toward him, the AR-15 off his shoulder now. Aiming.

And took an arrow through the heart, from the back.

It happened so fast, and yet in slow-motion, that Jane barely had time to register Beardo sagging before a movement on her right made her turn her bleary gaze to Tawny, striding in from the parking lot, pulling another from the quiver behind her back. Bow already locked for the next shot.

It was amazing to watch the smoothness of the motion, the fiery focus of the huntress's eyes, in the moment before the second arrow flew.

Then Jane turned back to the sound of screams, saw the big guy whirl and clutch at the glistening stick that now wore his left eye, dangling three inches from its socket.

Given another three-to-four seconds, it all might have turned out differently.

But, of course, it was the bony meth-head who pulled the trigger on his semi-automatic. Not even aiming. Just riddling the room as he spun, filling the air with red mist and bullet holes that the walls retained, all these many months later...

The blood and meat had been cleaned up, of course. She'd wanted to do it herself, felt the desperate need. Felt like she owed it to the people she'd lost, on her watch. But the survivors, and the crime-scene cops who showed up in the aftermath, all urged her to use professionals. "You don't need to put yourself through that," they said. "You have suffered enough."

Her broken response was, "Yeah. Like I fucking have money for that." But it was amazing, how her remaining friends and clientele, the families of the lost, and even strangers had come through for her. She barely knew the person who started the GoFundMe. But it topped the cost of the cleanup by nearly seven grand. (It was a national story, after all.)

The federal relief checks had helped immensely, too, for as long as they lasted. And her meagre savings had gotten her precisely this far.

But the coffers had run dry. She could barely afford the fucking lime for her last drink. The only asset of value she had was Calamity Jane's, which nobody would buy in this climate, even if she could bear to sell it.

Which was why she'd brought the handgun she wished she'd brought that night to the bar, tonight.

The bar suddenly filled with all these people she loved.

"But why?" she asked Tawny, seated at the bar beside her, both of them three drinks in.

"Oh, Janie. You know. It's like that thing we always talked about. Where a dog knows when its owner is coming home? Or it suddenly starts whimpering and pacing by the door, for what you think is no good reason..."

"And then you find out that its master just got hit by a car, twenty miles away..."

"Yeah. What's that called again?"

"The morphic field." As Jane's eyes widened.

"That's the shit," Tawny said, her own eyes gleaming the way they had when she took that final shot. Taking out the skinhead trash. As her own skull exploded, in their mutual closing act.

Jane couldn't stop the warm tears from flowing, as the warmth of the souls assembled gathered round. Surrounding her with an aura of peace.

"When we love hard enough," Tawny continued, "little things

like distance don't mean nothin'. Don't mean diddly. We're on each other's map. And that's forever."

"But…"

"We could feel you were about to do somethin' stupid, okay? It put a ripple in the field. Sent out the alert. And we couldn't let you do that without lettin' you know that you matter. Not just to us, but to a whole lotta people you opened your heart to. Cuz that's just the kind of slice of delicious, sweet-ass paradise you are."

The applause of the dead who could never truly die, because the best of our spirit lives on and on forever, too, filled the room and her bones and nerve endings with a feeling she'd feared she would never feel again.

A little thing called hope.

"Okay!" Jane said, raising her glass to the universe at large. "If you're gonna be that way about it…!"

"YAAAAAY!!!" hollered everybody.

In all our joy and sorrow, there ain't no morphic field like home.

SCREENPLAYS

Intro to
COME AS YOU ARE

The screenplay form is fascinating, and as far from prose as prose is from haiku. More like haiku, in fact, because the form is so rigid, and you have to say so much with so little. Economy of motion is key.

You are, in fact, limited to what you can see or hear. (In short, what is shootable for the camera, and playable for the actors.) And the formula runs to roughly one page per minute of film, or as close as you can get. Which runs entirely counter to the liberties novelists are accustomed to. Which is why so very few of them can write a good screenplay. (To my mind, William Goldman is the best, as witness his books and scripts for *Marathon Man*, *The Princess Bride*, and most particularly *Magic*.)

I love the form, myself. Probably because I'm a very cinematic writer to begin with, watching the movie in my head no matter what I'm writing. And also because I'm a director, and understand what the director, the producers, the cinematographer, the actors, the production designer, the wardrobe people, the makeup artists and fx artists and stuntmen or women, and everyone else -- down to the investors who write the checks -- need, in order to visualize what shows up on the screen.

This whacky Halloween party was intended for season 2 of Shudder's streaming series *Creepshow*, where I'd been lucky enough to land an episode in season 1 (*Times is Tough in Musky Holler*, with old friend Dori Miller).

They passed, alas -- too many monsters, just for starters -- but I had so much fun writing it that I just had to share.

So for those of you who wonder how screenplays work, HERE'S ONE NOW!

COME AS YOU ARE

Written by
John Skipp

EXT. BUSTER'S SUDS & BAR-B-Q - PARKING LOT - NIGHT

It's a beat-to-shit DIVE BAR on the outskirts of
town, under a NEARLY-FULL MOON. Paint peeled. Like
it's been out of business for years.

But inside, the LIGHTS ARE ON. Rockin' JUKEBOX
MUSIC can be heard from inside. And maybe a dozen
PICKUP TRUCKS, VANS, MUSCLE CARS, and a HEARSE are
already in the unpaved parking lot, surrounding a
MASSIVE FLAMING BARBECUE PIT.

And the ragged banner hanging across the front
porch reads:
PRIVATE HALLOWEEN BASH! COME AS YOU ARE!

                    DARREN(O.S.)
                So this is it?

                    KAREN (O.S.)
            Oh, honey, you better believe it is!

                                        CUT TO:

INT. DARREN'S CAR - PARKING LOT - CONTINUOUS - NIGHT

Behind the wheel is DARREN (30s, handsome) as they
pull in. In the passenger seat is KAREN (30's,
gorgeous). She's swigging from a CERAMIC FLASK. He
side-eyes her, grinning with clear attraction...

...and HITS A POTHOLE, lurching both of them forward and back.

> DARREN
>> Oops!

> KAREN
>> (laughing)
>> Keep your eye on the road, Romeo!

A SPRITZ OF BLOOD rolls down her chin as she grins
at him, VAMPIRE TEETH REVEALED.

> DARREN
>> I'm so sorry!

> KAREN
>> No worries, no hurries. You want some?

> DARREN
>> No, I'm good.

> KAREN
>> You like it fresh. I get it...oh,
>> there's Tanzie! HEY, TANZIE!

Through the windshield, as they pull up to the
front, TANZIE (20's) shuts the front door of the
bar behind her, waves, lights a smoke. She's AN-
OTHER HOT VAMPIRE, attired to entice.

And with her, lighting up, is WEASEL (50s), sporting ragged flannel and jeans. He has BEADY EYES and a WHISKERED RODENT SNOOT. If this is Halloween party makeup, it is really good.

The second Darren pulls to a stop, Karen's already out the door, racing toward Taznie, both of them squealing on their way to embrace.

Darren sighs, cuts the engine, and steps outside.

                                        CUT TO:

EXT. BUSTER'S FRONT PORCH - CONTINUOUS - NIGHT

Karen and Tanzie are just unhugging as Darren comes up the front steps. Tanzie eyeballs him appreciatively, as Weasel wipes PALE FOAM from his lips with one sleeve.

                    TANZIE
          Oh, and who is this handsome animal?

                    KAREN
          This is Darren. Who I like. So don't
          even think about it.

                    TANZIE
          Awww. Karen and Darren. That's so
          cute.

                    KAREN
          Right?

                    DARREN
          Hi.

                    WEASEL
          Karen and Darren, sittin' in a tree-

                    KAREN
          Jesus, Weasel.

                    WEASEL
          Just sayin'!

                    DARREN
               (proffering his hand)
          Hey.

                    WEASEL
          You might not wanna shake my hand,
          on account of the rabies and such.

                    TANZIE
          True story.

Darren withdraws his handshake offer, laughs. Everyone else does, too.

DARREN
Okay.

KAREN
How's it goin' in there?

TANZIE
Party's just gettin' started. But
you know how it is. This is gonna
be fucking great!

KAREN
Best party of the year. So, um, is
Joey here yet?

TANZIE
So far, so good.

KAREN
Sweet.
(to Darren)
Okay, baby. You ready to do this
thing?

In response, DARREN SWOOPS KAREN INTO A WORLD-
CLASS KISS. So hot, so connected that it's like
they're the only two creatures on Earth.

TANZIE
Whoa, shit!

Darren and Karen break the kiss, stare adoringly at each other.

> DARREN
>
> Oh yeah, I'm ready.

CUT TO:

INT. BUSTER'S BAR - CONTINUOUS - NIGHT

The first things they see, as they come in the front door, are BONITA (15) and ABUELA (150 years plus, but she still looks like she's 70).

Both of them GHOSTS who we can see through. Both smiling with delight.

> BONITA
>
> Oh, Karen!

> ABUELA
>
> Mi *favorita!*

> BONITA
>
> We would hug you if we could!

> KAREN
>
> Aw, come here...

Darren stands back, as they HUG THROUGH EACH OTHER in a threeway. Then helplessly looks around.

The inside of Buster's is as broke-down as the outside. There's DUST on the ANTIQUE NEON BEER CLOCK. Genuine COBWEBS everywhere. Like nobody's touched this place in 50 years.

Except this obviously isn't true. Because there are roughly 30 MONSTERS packing the BOOTHS that line the window wall, the TABLES in the center. And several grooving on the DANCE FLOOR near the JUKEBOX and the EMPTY STAGE at the back.

There are a couple more HOT VAMPIRES (of every sex). Innumerable GHOSTS, some dating back 100 years or more. Several ROTTING CORPSES, in full sentient zombie mode. But also STRANGER MONSTERS that fall out of neat categories. (A SKULL-HEADED WENDIGO with mean dance moves, swigging from a whiskey bottle, just for example.)

As Karen and the ghosts disengage, BUSTER THE BAR-TENDER (40's, latino) is clearly revealed behind the bar beyond them. Grinning.

> BUSTER
> Hey, baby! You made it!

> KAREN
> Like I wasn't gonna!

She's yelling to Buster, but grabs Darren's hand to drag him along toward the bar, as the ghosts part to either side.

                    KAREN (CONT'D)
                    (to Darren)
              Buster's the fucking best.

                                        CUT TO:

COMIC BOOK PAGES

Several panels depict BUSTER GETTING ROBBED by a
couple of DESPERATE GUNMEN. One POINTING A GUN.
The other moving behind the bar to the kitchen. As
he hollers, standing his ground.

                    KAREN (V.O.)
              He got murdered back in 1976,
              during a robbery gone wrong. The
              same one that killed Bonita and
              Abuela.

The next panels show Abuela at the sink, washing
dishes, HANDS UP IN SURPRISE at the gunman's
approach. Then Bonita hiding behind the stove,
crying, as ABUELA IS SHOT IN THE EYE.

                    DARREN (V.O.)
              Shit...

The last panels show BUSTER SCREAMING RAGE. Then
BONITA LOOKING UP IN TERROR at the GUN POINTED AT

HER. A shot behind the bar, as BUSTER REACHES FOR HIS SHOTGUN. And a panel marked BLAM!

> KAREN (V.O.)
> Yeah, it was horrible...

                                            CUT TO:

INT. BUSTER'S BAR - CONTINUOUS - NIGHT

Karen and Darren reach the bar.

> KAREN
> But life is horrible, right?

> BUSTER
> Last time I checked! But hey, you take the good with the bad, you know?
>
> (shouting down the bar)
> Hey, Lucius! A pitcher of *Michelada con Sangre* for the lady!

> KAREN
> I love you.
> (to Darren)
> C'mon.

                                            CUT TO:

COMIC STRIP PAGES

The first panel is of LUCIUS (30s, odd), behind the
bar. The second is a matching shot of Lucius (8,
still odd). Both versions wearing the same SUIT,
BUTTON-DOWN SHIRT, AND BOWTIE. In both, he has the
same DEAD EYES.

> KAREN (V.O.)
> Lucius is sort of a local legend
> here in St. George County.

> DARREN (V.O.)
> Okay...

Next panels show him -- with the same clinical
expression -- DROWNING HIS OLDER SISTER IN THE
BATHTUB. At 8 years old. Using a TOILET PLUNGER to
hold her head down.

> KAREN (V.O.)
> Classic psychopath. If he wasn't
> rich, they'd have caught him by now.

> DARREN (V.O.)
> Sounds like a classic asshole.

> KAREN (V.O.)
> Yeah. Except she was worse. And all
> the things she did to him, they
> both learned from mom and dad.

Next panel is of his HORRIBLE, LEERING PARENTS,
looking down at him with something between hunger
and pride. Next is him looking up -- FRIGHTENING
SMALL by comparison -- somewhere between fear and
optimism. Dripping plunger still in hand.

MOM'S WORD BALLOON: "Well done, my son."

DAD'S WORD BALLOON: "There may be hope for you
yet."

CUT TO:

INT. BUSTER'S BAR - CONTINUOUS

Now Karen and Darren are standing behind OGRE
(60's), a MALFORMED FOUR-ARMED HULK with THREE
PITCHES OF BEER before him. Lucius still pouring
the fourth from one of many TAPS.

> KAREN
> The good news is, he's an excellent
> brewer and mixologist. And every
> year, he foots the bill on this
> shindig. So drinks are on the house
> tonight. He's a true friend of the
> monster community.

> OGRE
> (picking up four pitchers)
> Roog.

Ogre steps away from the bar, clearing the way to
Lucius.

                    LUCIUS
          Ah, Miss Karen. Lovely to see you.

                    KAREN
          Always a pleasure. So what have you
          got for us tonight?

                    LUCIUS
          The Honey Maggot IPA is a robust
          blend of regional hops and barley,
          with watermelon honey, and just the
          tiniest hint of maggot.

Darren winces. Karen laughs.

                    KAREN
          Probably not for us.

                    LUCIUS
          The Chocolate Habanero Skullfuck
          Stout came out exceptionally well
          this year. But that may be too rich
          for your tastes.

                    KAREN
          Yeah. So what's your lightest and
          brightest?

                    LUCIUS
                (almost smiling)
            For you, I have brewed a Pituitary
            Pilsner so clear it is almost
            transcendent, to tickle your
            Infinity Gland.

                    KAREN
            Ah, you know me too well. Let's
            start with that. And...?

Lucius takes a pitcher, starts tapping a golden
stream. And nods toward the taps on the far right.

                    LUCIUS
            Tonight, you've got your pick of
            locally-sourced and disease-free
            Rapist Red, or the traditional
            Virgin Spring.

                    KAREN
                (to Darren)
            Whaddaya think? Nasty vengeance, or
            innocent blood?

                    DARREN
            I mean, it's your call. But
            honestly, innocence always makes me
            sad.

                    KAREN
          Okay! Rapist Red it is! And fuck
          those fucking guys!

Lucius nods, stops the golden flow, and slides the
half-full pitcher down to the furthest tap.

POURING BLOOD IN, from the full keg below, to mix
with the beer.

                    KAREN (CONT'D)
          Oooo. Isn't that pretty?

Suddenly, LOUD MOTORCYCLE ROARS ERUPT FROM OUT-
SIDE. And everyone turns, including Darren. The
only one who doesn't know what that means.

                    KAREN (CONT'D)
          Oboy...

                    DARREN
          What?

                    KAREN
          Grab the pitcher, would'ja? Let's
          get a table, while we still can.

Darren nods as she grabs a pair of glasses and
starts walking. Lucius watches her go, slides the
pitcher over, and looks him dead in the eyes.

                    LUCIUS
          I don't know what manner of monster
          you are. And past a touch of mild
          intellectual curiosity on my part,
          I completely don't care.

                    DARREN
          Well, thanks for sharing. Guess
          psychosis is its own reward.

                    LUCIUS
          Oh, she told you? Good. I hope she
          told you what you're in for.

                    DARREN
          She told me this was gonna be a
          blast. And I believe her.

                    LUCIUS
          Well, then, good luck with that.

                    DARREN
          I make my own luck, Lucius. Thanks
          for the beer.

With that, Darren turns, sees Karen waving to him
from the table closest to the dance floor. Notes
the monsters eyeballing him with curiosity as he
passes. Nods and smiles as he goes.

          AT THE TABLE

Karen is sitting with CLOVUS (an ancient DEMON) and ANYA (a grizzled GHOST OF A WITCH dating back to the 1800's). They're both drunk and happy.

> CLOVUS
> ...but anti-CHRIST, I can't tell ya how nice it is to have a fucking night off!

> ANYA
> Aye! 'Tis a mercy indeed to cease with the haunting and frightening and cursing and dooming, if only for a day!

Clovus and Anya cackle together, CLINK SPIRIT GLASSES, as Darren sets the pitcher down and sits beside Karen.

> KAREN
> You're just in time!

> DARREN
> (pouring)
> What did I miss?

                                        CUT TO:

COMIC BOOK PAGES

The first panel is an OLD VICTORIAN HAUNTED HOUSE.
Old as Anya. With a BLAZING PYRE BEFORE IT.
Second panel is a closeup of the blaze, with ANYA
SCREAMING INSIDE IT.

> KAREN (V.O.)
> Well, Anya was the first one to
> curse this place. So she's the OG
> of St. George County, unless you
> count the Wendigo. Which I totally
> do.

The next panels show ANYA FRIGHTENING 200 YEARS OF
CHILDREN. One prank after another. As child after
child SCREAMS. Each frame generationally updating
the background of the same bedroom, in the same
house.

> KAREN (V.O.)
> But the bad news is, she has to
> haunt the same stupid house
> forever. Doing the same thing, over
> and over.

The next panels abruptly pivot to CLOVUS, BURNING
IN HELL AND GRINNING. As tormented souls suffer
behind him.

> KAREN (V.O.)
> Clovus, on the other hand, is older
> than God.

                    CLOVUS (V.O.)
          Almost.

The next panels show a POSSESSED WOMAN TIED TO A
BED, EXORCIST-STYLE. In the first, she's a teen-
ager. In the second, she's middle-aged. In the
third, she looks almost as old as Anya.

                    KAREN (V.O.)
          But then Satan compelled him to
          possess little Peggy Ann Reed, who
          should have been easy pickings.
          Except she's hung on for sixty
          years and counting!

The next panels show ONE EXORCIST AFTER ANOTHER,
DROPPING DEAD. And poor Clovus, looking increasingly desperate as every attempt to free him
fails.

                                        CUT TO:

INT. BUSTER'S BAR - CONTINUOUS
Everybody at the table's eyes on Clovus.

                    CLOVUS
          And, I mean, it's hard. You know? I
          mean, everybody's got their shitty
          job they gotta do. But this shit is
          taking forever. You know?

> ANYA
> 'Tis a very long time.

> DARREN
> So why are you here, instead of
> there?

EVERYBODY LAUGHS, except Darren.

> KAREN
> Because it's Halloween, Goofy! And
> in St. George County, that means we
> get to take the night off. Let all
> the amateur mortal civilians of the
> world pretend they're us for the
> night. Dress up like us. Wish they
> were this cool.

At which point, in the distance, THE FRONT DOOR
BLOWS OPEN.

And in strides JOEY (30's, handsome and dangerous), leading his HAIRY BIKER GANG.

> JOEY
> WOOOOOO!!! Is this shit on or what?

JOEY AND KAREN LOCK EYES, from all across the
room. Then JOEY LOCKS EYES WITH DARREN. Nods. And
starts rapidly approaching.

Darren starts to stand. Karen stops him.

                    KAREN
              Hang on, baby.

He turns to her. Nails her with his eyes. Cups her
face tenderly in his hands.

In that moment, for the first time, she looks sur-
prisingly vulnerable. Like she only has eyes for
him.

Which is totally disgusting to Joey, as he comes
up to their table.

                    JOEY
              Seriously, Karen?

                    KAREN
              Joey, give it a rest, okay?

                    JOEY
              I mean, you wanna get me all
              green-eyed and mean, you might hafta
              do better than that.

                    KAREN
              Ha! Like I give a fuck what you
              think!

                    JOEY
         Well, then I guess you don't mind
         if I mop the parking lot with his
         pretty little sissy-ass face.

Now it's Darren's turn to laugh.

                 JOEY (CONT'D)
         Oh, you think that's funny?

                   DARREN
         It's gonna get funnier in a minute.

The crowd, which is watching all this, goes...

                  THE CROWD
         OOOOOOOOO!

                    JOEY
         Okay, Bozo! Let's take your clown
         car for a spin!

                  THE CROWD
         DOG FIGHT! DOG FIGHT!

And as Darren stands, DOZENS OF OTHERS DO, TOO.
Until it's a parade toward the door, with Joey in
the lead.

Leaving Karen at the table with Anya, surrounded
by mostly ghosts. Shaking her head resignedly.

Then SWIGGING HER GLASS OF BLOODY BEER. And
standing as well.

                                        CUT TO:

EXT. BUSTER'S FRONT PORCH - CONTINUOUS

Tanzie and Weasel are still on the porch, smoking,
as Karen comes out.

                    TANZIE
            That didn't take long.

                    KAREN
            Uh-huh. Got a smoke?

Weasel reaches for his pack. Karen shakes her head
no, then turns as Tanzie offers her one and lights
it.

                                        CUT TO:

EXT. BUSTER'S SUDS & BAR-B-Q - PARKING LOT
- CONTINUOUS

Meanwhile, a FIGHT CIRCLE has formed around DARREN
AND JOEY, as they begin to square off under the
NEARLY-FULL MOON.

JOEY'S WOLFEN EYES GLOW. And he has a FULL SET OF
FANGS.

                    JOEY
          You're just lucky it ain't a full
          moon, bitch!

                    DARREN (O.S.)
          Full enough for me.

                                        CUT TO:

          COMIC BOOK PAGES

These panels track DARREN'S TRANSFORMATION INTO
A WERE-TIGER. Striped fur. Feline eyes. Fearsome
fangs. And razor claws.

Still humanoid in form. But terrifying as hell.

                                        CUT TO:

EXT. BUSTER'S SUDS & BAR-B-Q - PARKING LOT
- CONTINUOUS

Suddenly, Joey looks a lot less confident.

                    JOEY
          Oh, shit.

That's when WERE-TIGER DARREN POUNCES, DRAGGING
JOEY DOWN so fast he doesn't even have a chance.

In an instant, DARREN'S TEETH ARE ON JOEY'S

THROAT, amidst a MASSIVE BLOOD SPRAY. Joey
howling. Darren digging in...

...until JOEY'S HEAD COMES OFF, and tumbles sideways. Landing upside-down.

As the CROWD GOES WILD.

> JOEY'S HEAD
> Goddamit.

> WEASEL
> More meat for the barbecue!

> THE CROWD
> WOOOOOOO!!!

And nobody applauds more fiercely than Karen.

CUT TO:

INT. BUSTER'S BAR - CONTINUOUS

The crowd pours back in, chipper, except for the
MOURNUL BIKERS who file in, lamenting the loss of
their Alpha male.

Darren's back to his full-human self. And Karen's
wrapped around him, giddy.

KAREN

And you can do that any time you
want?

DARREN
(purring)
Any time you want.

KAREN
(purring back)
Oh, honey!

As they sweep past, we see JOEY THE GHOST back at
the bar, with Buster.

BUSTER
Hey, sorry, bruh. It had to happen
sometime.

JOEY THE GHOST
Yeah. Fuck it. What'choo got on
tap?

Suddenly, a LOUD GUITAR TWANG turns everybody's
heads toward the STAGE, at the back.

SLOW POISONER (O.S.)
LAY-DEEEES AND GENTLE-CREATURES!

CUT TO:

INT. BUSTER'S STAGE - CONTINUOUS

Where the stage was once empty, it now bears an
ENORMOUS FIBERBOARD DEMON HEAD, garishly and
creepily painted. Surrounding it are CREEPY FI-
BERBOARD TREES, with HOWLING FACES in the trunks
beneath their bare branches.

And through the GAPING DEMON MOUTH -- from the
blackness beyond -- steps THE SLOW POISONER (40s).

He's wearing a traditional black UNDERTAKER'S
SUIT, but with ORANGE NEON TRIM.

And as he grins sardonically at the audience, the
AUDIENCE WILDLY APPLAUDS.

                    SLOW POISONER
               Once again we gather, on this most
               auspicious occasion, to celebrate
               the one and only holiday that
               honors us, here at the hallowed
               Buster's Suds and Barbecue!

                    THE CROWD
                 (wildly applauding)
               WOOOOOOO!!!!

> SLOW POISONER
> For many of us, this is the only
> night of the year that we are
> allowed or otherwise able to come
> together, commingle, exchange trade
> secrets and bodily or ectoplasmic
> fluids...

Laughs and hoots from the crowd.

> SLOW POISONER (CONT'D)
> ...and this is a wild and beautiful
> thing. Because we are, in fact,
> those wild and beautiful things! So
> are you ready to commingle,
> brothers and sisters and mysterious
> others?

> THE CROWD
> WOOOOOO!!!

A FLASH POT GOES OFF on mid-stage. And when the
fire and smoke clear, The Slow Poisoner has a BLACK
SQUID-SHAPED ELECTRIC GUITAR in his hands. And a
BASS DRUM at his feet, with the words "THE SLOW
POISONER" emblazoned upon it.

> SLOW POISONER
> Then LET THE MAYHEM BEGIN!

And with that, he launches into a FEROCIOUS

PSYCHOBILLY ONEMAN-BAND PERFORMANCE, at breakneck
pace.

                                        CUT TO:

INT. BUSTER'S DANCE FLOOR - MONTAGE - CONTINUOUS

Karen and Darren join the MAD RUSH, instantly
grooving with each other to the crazy beat.

But pretty much everyone in Buster's is gettin'
down on the floor now. Witches dancing with demons.
Vampires dancing with biker werewolves. Ghosts
mostly dancing with each other. Zombies dancing
badly.

This is the "Monster Mash" incarnate: the monster
party we always wanted to see. Sexy. Freaky. Full
of dozens of visual jokes.

And is it goes on -- from song to song -- it just
gets DRUNKER AND CRAZIER. Our gaze veering and
smearing, for roughly TWO MINUTES of nightmare
shenanigans.

Even Lucius, behind the bar, is lightly grooving
and allowing himself half a smile.

And as the last song draws to a close, A LOUD BELL
STARTS CLANGING FROM OUTSIDE.

                    SLOW POISONER
                    A-ha! The dinner bell rings! Which
                    gives us a few last precious
                    moments to step back, and remember
                    who we are. And who we were.

He begins a SLOW, SORROWFUL SONG.

And everyone tunes in, feeling it in this moment.

[NOTE: This song isn't written yet. But these
lyrics are intended to give a sense of the tone
and message.]

                    SLOW POISONER (CONT'D)
                         (singing)
                    We were born. And then we died.
                    Nobody cared. Nobody cried. So we
                    became the things we came to be.

Karen and Darren look deep into each other, pull
each other into a sweet SLOW DANCE.

                    SLOW POISONER (CONT'D)
                         (singing)

                    So we prey, through all our days.
                    Till it all becomes a haze. Just
                    praying against prayer to be set
                    free.

Now others begin to dance as well.

                    SLOW POISONER (CONT'D)
                         (singing)
                    To live forever is a blessing and a
                    curse. To do our best while our
                    fate says "Do your worst." It's an
                    impossible task, and it never ends.

And Karen is not the only one OPENLY WEEPING NOW.
Even the ones who aren't dancing are HUGGING each
other, or crying into their beverage of choice.

And it's comical, yes. But also beautiful, sad,
and true. An unexpected overflowing of real
emotion.

So when they get to the chorus, it is no surprise
that many of them start SINGING ALONG. This is a
song that they know.

                    EVERYBODY
                         (singing)
                    WE ARE MONSTERS! WE ARE CREATURES!
                    WE ALL HAVE OUR OWN WEIRD FEATURES!
                    WE WEAR DIFFERENT MASKS! WE HAVE
                    DIFFERENT TASKS! WE HAVE DIFFERENT
                    FATES AS OUR HELL AWAITS!

Now even Darren has tears in his eyes, caught up
in the moment.

                    EVERYBODY (CONT'D)
                      (singing)
           WE ARE MONSTERS! WE ARE DOOMED! BUT
           HERE'S TO EVERY LOST SOUL IN THE
           ROOM!

And The Slow Poisoner PAUSES, lets the moment
hang. Then continues alone.

                    SLOW POISONER
                   (singing a cappela)
           From near and far, come as you
           are...

Then he launches into FULL-TILT PSYCHOBILLY DANCE
MODE. As the CROWD GOES WILD.

                    SLOW POISONER (CONT'D)
                      (singing loud)
           MY NIGHTMARE FRIENDS!

                    EVERYBODY
           MY NIGHTMARE FRIENDS!

                    SLOW POISONER
           MY TERRIFYING FRIENDS!

                    EVERYBODY
           MY NIGHTMARE FRIENDS!

                    SLOW POISONER
              MY VERY VERY BEST FRIENDS!

                    EVERYBODY
                  (even Darren)
              MY NIGHTMARE FRIENDS!

And with that, he brings the song to a THRILL-
PACKED CLOSE FULL OF HOWLING APPLAUSE.

                                        CUT TO:

EXT. BUSTER'S SUDS & BAR-B-Q - PARKING LOT

The whole crowd is gathered around the GIANT BAR-
BECUE PIT. Where BARBECUED HUMAN RIBS and LIMBS
and other choice parts are being parsed out and
shared.

On the outskirts, Karen and Darren are snuggling.

                    KAREN
              So was I right or what?

                    DARREN
              Oh, yeah. Best monster party
              ever...shhhh.

He turns toward the WOODS surrounding the parking
lot.

                                        CUT TO:

EXT. WOODS OUTSIDE PARKING LOT - CONTINUOUS

There are SEVERAL HUMAN CHILDREN -- dressed in
HALLOWEEN GARB -- staring out from behind the
trees in terror, excitement, and awe.

                                        CUT TO:

EXT. BUSTER'S SUDS & BAR-B-Q - PARKING LOT - CON-
TINUOUS As WERE-DARREN and FULL-FANGED KAREN turn
to the children.

                    KAREN AND DARREN
              Boo!

                                        CUT TO:

EXT. WOODS OUTSIDE PARKING LOT - CONTINUOUS

As the CHILDREN SHRIEK AND RUN AWAY.

                                        CUT TO:

EXT. BUSTER'S SUDS & BAR-B-Q - PARKING LOT
- CONTINUOUS

As Karen and Darren LAUGH.

                    DARREN
          Yeah! Run, you little bastards!

                    KAREN
          Aw, come on! They're cute!

                    DARREN
          That's why it's so much fun!

                    KAREN
          Right?

They kiss quick, then both grin at the camera.

               KAREN AND DARREN
          Happy Halloweeen, everybody!

Then the camera sweeps back to include the ENTIRE
MONSTER CROWD. All smiling at the camera, and our
audience, as well.

                  EVERYBODY
          HAAAAAAAPPY HALLOWEEEEEEEEEN!!!

And as they wave and cheer, we...

                              FADE TO BLACK.

Intro to
STINKLEBERRIES

Writing for television is tough, even if you've got an in. Like feature films, the dollar-to-dream ratio tends to err on the side of the money.

That said, when my good friend Rose O'Keefe and I took a drive up Mt. Hood to the Timberline Lodge (home of the exteriors for the Overlook Hotel in Kubrick's version of THE SHINING), we had a stinkleberry incident much like the one described here. Albeit, thank God, with less mutation and heartbreak.

And though I knew it was too expensive to submit to *Creepshow*, I had to write it anyway, just for fun. And -- as with *Come As You Are* -- boy, would I looooove to shoot this crazy thing sometime!

STINKLEBERRIES

Written by
John Skipp

EXT. OREGON MOUNTAIN ROAD - DAY

Beautiful trees turning color on a sweeping vista,
so high up it gives you vertigo to look. We track
DUSTY'S BEAT-UP LAND ROVER from above as it nego-
tiates the sweeping turns along the edge of ma-
jestic MT. HOOD.

                                        CUT TO:

INT. CAR - DAY

DUSTY (mid-30s, trans-female) is behind the wheel.
DAWN (mid-20s, cis female) is riding shotgun,
PHONE in hand.

The BACK SEAT IS PACKED WITH SUITCASES AND FILM
GEAR. And there's a stack of PROMOTIONAL MATERIALS
for a movie called "You Will Not Deny Us". Written
by, directed, and starring the two of them.

Dawn sighs wearily, sets the phone in her lap.
LIGHTS A JOINT, and takes a deep toke.

                    DAWN
          Okay. So they want us to stupid it
          up.

                    DUSTY
          Yep. Like the story's not simple
          enough.

                    DAWN
          Girl meets girl. Girl loses girl.
          Girl gets girl. Throw a boy in
          there, and that's every romantic
          comedy of the last 10,000 years.

                    DUSTY
          Yeah, but throw a trans-girl in,
          and-

                    DAWN
          Suddenly it's bizarro science
          fiction.

                    DUSTY
          With a tragic ending. Don't forget.

                    DAWN
          Fuck that.

Dawn takes another toke, then leans over and PULLS
DUSTY'S FACE TO HERS IN A KISS. Blowing the smoke
into Dusty, who EXHALES IT OUT HER NOSE. So we
know it worked.

                    DUSTY
          Mmmm. Thank you.

                    DAWN
          Dusty? It's only cuz I love you.

                    DUSTY
          Dawn, baby, I love you, too, but-

                    DAWN
          But that's not enough. They need a
          fucking stinkleberry-

Dusty guffaws. She has a giant laugh.

                    DUSTY
          A what?

                    DAWN
               (laughing, too)
          You know! A stinkleberry! Like we
          made this beautiful, perfect fruit
          salad, and they said, "This is
          great, but it doesn't stink enough.
          Could you maybe throw in a couple
          stinkleberries?"

                    DUSTY
          HAW HAW HAW! Yeah! Okay. So like
          they fall in love-

                    DAWN
          But their love is a tumor. So
          they're exiled to Cancervania, a
          magical kingdom that's actually a
          queendom-

                    DUSTY
But they're not welcome there
either-

                    DAWN
Because they've only grown three
tumor-heads, and you need a minimum
of five to get in-

                    DUSTY
But-

                    DAWN
But their love is so strong that
they grow hundreds of tumor-heads
of each other on their own bodies.
Then merge into one-

                    DUSTY
And become the new queen of
Cancervania! I love it!

                    DAWN
Right? Now that's a fucking movie
I'd pay money to see!

                    DUSTY
I love a happy ending. Let's make
that one instead!

                    DAWN
             (passing the joint)
          WOOOOO!!!

                    DUSTY
             (toking)
          Except - pfff -- they'd never
          finance it.

                    DAWN
          They might not finance this one.

Dusty exhales a plume of smoke, nods sourly,
passes the joint back.

                    DUSTY
          Not enough stinkleberries. Speaking
          of which, I need to poop something
          fierce.

                    DAWN
          Right? What was in those burritos?

They both bust up laughing.

                    DUSTY AND DAWN
             STINKLEBERRIES!

                                        CUT TO:

EXT. MOUNTAIN ROAD - DAY

As their car drives further down Mt. Hood, toward
the landbelow.

>   DUSTY (O.S.)
>   (farting)
>   They were pretty good, though.

>   DAWN
>   Jesus! Open the window!

>   CUT TO:

EXT. DINER PARKING LOT - DAY
Dusty and Dawn are parked maybe ten cars away from
the ENTRANCE. Walking toward the front door. Both
with phones in hand.

>   DAWN
>   Okay. So it's just another ten
>   miles-

>   DUSTY
>   And shit. Jerry says he wants
>   rewrites by Wednesday at the
>   latest.

>   DAWN
>   Aw, come on! Are you serious?

They don't notice the HUDDLED COUPLE staggering
up the sidewalk toward them from behind. A ragtag
couple, holding each other close. Possibly homeless. Possibly campers in the wilderness. But only
seen from a distance.

                                        CUT TO:

INT. DINER BATHROOM HALLWAY - DAY

Dusty's walking a little faster, desperately
heading for the LADIES ROOM DOOR.

                    DUSTY
          Sorry. Age before beauty.

                    DAWN
          You're a beauty to me!

Dusty reaches the door, sees the OCCUPIED SIGN
above the doorknob, hears the TOILET FLUSHING.

                    DUSTY
          Oh, c'mon c'mon c'mon...

Directly across the hall is the MEN'S ROOM DOOR.
Which reads VACANT. They both look at it.

                    DUSTY (CONT'D)
          I don't go there any more.

Dawn draws her close for another kiss.

                    DAWN
              Why would you?

THE LADIES ROOM DOOR OPENS, just as they kiss
right in front of it.

A RUGGED, RUSTIC OLDER WOMAN (BRENDA, 50s)
freezes, looks at them in first shock, then
judgment.

                    DUSTY
              Oh, sorry. Next!

Brenda steps back as Dusty pushes through. Leaving
Dawn and Brenda standing there, in frank eye
contact.

                    DAWN
              Hey. When you gotta go, you gotta
              go. Hope that's not a problem.

                    BRENDA
              Is she, uh...

                    DAWN
              My girlfriend, yeah.

                    BRENDA

Oh, honey. She's not anyone's girlfriend.

           DAWN
Lady, I think I'll be the judge of
that.

           BRENDA
          (disgusted)
She's not even a real woman.

           DAWN
Oh, yeah? Then you're not even a
real human.

Brenda goes livid, brings one hand up to SLAP.
Dawn brings her LEFT up to BLOCK, pulls her RIGHT
up to PUNCH, in full martial arts stance.

           DAWN (CONT'D)
Oh, you don't wanna do that.

Brenda backs off, bristling.

           BRENDA
You're lucky I don't have my gun.

           DAWN
You're lucky I don't have mine.

           BRENDA
          (storming off)

You better hope I never see you again!

                    DAWN
              That sounds great! Bye!

Dawn watches Brenda tromp up the stairs. Hears the
FRONT DOOR TINKLE OPEN (bells on the door), then
SLAM. She grins. Opens the Ladies Room door. And
steps inside. Door swinging shut.

                  DAWN (O.S.) (CONT'D)
                  (coughing, laughing)
              JESUS CHRIST!

                    DUSTY (O.S.)
              SORRY!

                                        CUT TO:

EXT. DINER PARKING LOT - DAY

Dusty and Dawn walk back to their car, both
staring at their phones again. They barely notice
the HUDDLED COUPLE till they're almost upon them.

                    DUSTY
              Oops! Sorry!

                  HUDDLED COUPLE
                  (in unison)
              'Scuse me.

The Huddled Couple have HOODIES pulled down, so we
can barely see their faces. But their FACES LOOK
WRONG. WEIRDLY PUFFY, in the brief glimpse we get.

And they also SMELL TERRIBLE, as witnessed by the
wincing expressions on Dusty's and Dawn's faces as
they stare at each other, watch the couple pass.
Then walk away, as fast as possible.

                    DAWN
          Phew!

                    DUSTY
               (waving her hands)
          Holy Jesus!

                    DAWN
               (laughing)
          How many months between showers do
          you think that would take?

                    DUSTY
          I feel so bad for them. But-

                    DAWN
          There but for the grace of Goddess
          go-

                    DUSTY
          Hang on. What's that?

As they come upon their car, they see...

                                        CUT TO:

EXT ECU CLOSEUP - CAR'S VENTILATION DUCTS

Right between the windshield wipers and the front
of the hood, we see LITTLE BROKEN CLUMPS OF
BROWNISH FRUIT. Sitting right on the ducts. Sprin-
kled all the way across.

                                        CUT TO:

EXT. DINER PARKING LOT - DAY

Dusty and Dawn stare at them.

                    DAWN
          I don't know.

                    DUSTY
          They're like miniature apricots or
          something. Did we park under some
          weird tree?

There are no trees in the parking lot. And no
other fruits on the hood of the car.

                    DAWN
          Maybe back on Mt. Tabor?

                    DUSTY
         Whatever-

Dusty matter-of-factly PLUCKS SEVERAL CLUMPS from
the ducts, tosses them into the parking lot behind
her.

                    DAWN
              Ewwww-

                    DUSTY
         You wanna help out, you could do
         the other side.

                    DAWN
         No, I'm good.

                    DUSTY
         I'll get the rest later. You ready?

                    DAWN
         Open my door already!

                                        CUT TO:

INT. CAR - DAY

Dusty backs up, drives out of the parking lot onto
the road. And immediately WRINKLES HER NOSE in
disgust. Dawn does, too.

> DUSTY
> Oof! What the hell?

> DAWN
> Did you step in some puke or
> something?

> DUSTY
> No!

> DAWN
> Cuz it smells like a drunk tank at
> closing time!

> DUSTY
> I know! Gaaaaah!

They quickly ROLL DOWN THE WINDOWS. Dawn sticks
her head out hers, taking some fresh breaths before coming back in.

> DUSTY (CONT'D)
> Is that better?

> DAWN
> I don't know. No.

Dawn leans forward, sniffs the nearest DASHBOARD
AIR VENT, and nearly pukes.

                    DAWN (CONT'D)
            Urgh! Pull over!

                        DUSTY
            What?

Dawn leans back out the window, and VIOLENTLY
VOMITS all over the road, down the side of the
door.

                        DAWN
            Goddamit!

                        DUSTY
            Oh, baby! Shit!

DUSTY PULLS OFF TO THE SHOULDER, SLAMS ON THE
BRAKES.

                                    CUT TO:

EXT. MOUNTAIN ROAD - DAY

The second they stop, DAWN THROWS OPEN THE DOOR.
Stagger three steps before collapsing to her
knees, and DRY-HEAVES. Panting. Tears running down
her face.

One CAR DOOR SLAM LATER, Dusty comes rushing up
from behind. She's got a ROLL OF PAPER TOWELS in

one hand, A BOTTLE OF WATER in the other.

                    DUSTY
          I'm here, Dawn. I'm here.

Dawn lets Dusty WIPE HER CHIN with a paper towel,
feed her some water from the bottle. Dawn GARGLES
the water, swooshes it around in her mouth, and
spits it out.

                    DAWN
          Oh, those motherfuckers-

                    DUSTY
          Which ones?

                    DAWN
          I don't know if it was those stinky
          hitchhiking motherfuckers, or that
          bitch from the bathroom, or some
          other random asshole-

                    DUSTY
          But-

                    DAWN
          But that shit on your grill didn't
          just land randomly. There were no
          tiny apricots on your hood.

                    DUSTY
          Somebody deliberately put that shit
          on there. Yeah.

                    DAWN
          Actual stinkleberries.

                    DUSTY
          I'm really starting to hate this
          story.

Dusty helps Dawn up, and they stagger back to the
car. Bypassing the puked-up door toward the hood.

                    DAWN
          Gimme a towel.

Dusty tears one off, hands it over. Dawn takes it,
folds it double, and PLUCKS SEVERAL STINKLEBERRIES
off the vents.

The last of them SQUISHES as she plucks it up, a
SYRUPY STRINGER TRAILING UP FROM THE VENT.

                    DAWN (CONT'D)
          Ewww-

                    DUSTY
          Hang on-

Dusty wets a paper towel, nudges Dawn aside, and
MOPS UP THE VENT. Scrubbing it clean. Getting
every last drop or speck.

                    DUSTY (CONT'D)
              We got this.

                    DAWN
              Okay. Lemme do the door at least.
              I'm so sorry-

                    DUSTY
              You didn't do anything wrong. We
              didn't do anything wrong.

                                        CUT TO:

INT. CAR - DAY

They are driving again. Windows down. And both of
them looking sickly.

                    DUSTY
              That's better, right?

                    DAWN
              Yeah. But it's still not great. How
              you feeling?

                    DUSTY

Like shit. Like my brain is foggy And-

She takes her right hand off the wheel, rubs it against her pants leg.

> DUSTY (CONT'D)
> I feel itchy.

Dawn rubs her sleeve against her nose.

> DAWN
> Yeah. Me, too.

> DUSTY
> If this is like a spore, it could get into the upholstery.

> DAWN
> And our luggage.

> DUSTY
> And our gear. Shit!

> DAWN
> You got any spray disinfectant in the trunk?

> DUSTY
> No. But we could hit a drug store.

> DAWN

If there is one between here and there.
We're up in the fucking mountains-

> DUSTY

A gas station mini-mart.

> DAWN

Wouldn't hold my breath.

> DUSTY

I'm holding my breath already. But
worse come to worst, they'll
probably have some there. How far
away is it now?

> DAWN

Maybe fifteen minutes?

> DUSTY

Okay...

CUT TO:

EXT. MOUNTAIN ROAD - SUNSET

The sky is gorgeous, as are the woods to either
side. But DUSTY'S CAR SWERVES OVER THE YELLOW
LINE, veers back abruptly, NARROWLY AVOIDS A CAR
coming the other way.

                    DUSTY (O.S.)
          Shit!

                                      CUT TO:

INT. CAR - SUNSET - CONTINUOUS

Dusty grapples the wheel with her left hand,
because her RIGHT HAND IS RIDDLED WITH SWOLLEN
BUMPS.

Beside her, Dawn moans. Her RIGHT EYE, NOSE, AND
FOREHEAD are all SWOLLEN TOGETHER into a BULBOUS
BUMPY RIDGE, like a unibrow slung all the way down
to her cheek.

Off to their right, the first of several A-FRAME
COTTAGES appear through the dense woods.

                    DUSTY
          Is this it?

Dawn looks at her phone with her one good eye.

                    DAWN
          In five hundred feet, turn right.

                                      CUT TO:

EXT. A-FRAME COTTAGE - SUNSET - CONTINUOUS

Down the long DRIVEWAY they go, through copious
trees, to the BEAUTIFUL COTTAGE at the end. Lights
on inside. Welcoming.

There's another LAND ROVER parked by the back of
the house. Dusty pulls up in front. Cuts the engine. Gets out.

                    DUSTY
          I'll be back in a minute, okay?
          Just wanna make sure we're good.

She shuts the door, advances to the FRONT PORCH.
Opens up the MAILBOX with her good hand. Finds the
KEYS. And UNLOCKS THE FRONT DOOR.

                                        CUT TO:

INT. A-FRAME COTTAGE - LIVING ROOM - CONTINUOUS

Dusty steps inside. It's beautiful. Rustic.
There's a FIREPLACE at the back and center, logs
stacked and ready to go. Above it is a GUN RACK,
with SEVERAL HUNTING RIFLES displayed.

                    DUSTY
          Oh, this is perfect.

From the KITCHEN, in the distance, comes a
CLINKING SOUND.

                    WOMAN'S VOICE (O.S.)
                    Hello?

                         DUSTY
                    (surprised)
                    Oh, hi! We're your renters! We're
                    here!

                    WOMAN'S VOICE (O.S.)
                    I'm sorry! I'm just finishing up!
                    I'll be gone before you know it!

Dusty nervously backs toward the front door.
Looking at her MALFORMED ARM. Looking worse by the
second. TUMORS PULSING.

                         DUSTY
                    No worries! We'll be out front!

                    WOMAN'S VOICE (O.S.)
                    Hang on! I'll be right there,
                    honey!

Dusty freezes, hiding her bad hand behind her, as
FOOTSTEPS APPROACH.

From the kitchen, BRENDA APPEARS. Big friendly
smile on her face.

>   BRENDA
>   It's always nice to greet my
>   guests, and-

THEY SEE EACH OTHER. And Brenda freezes in shock.

>   BRENDA (CONT'D)
>   Oh, hell no.

>   DUSTY
>   What?

>   BRENDA
>   You are not staying here.

>   DUSTY
>   I'm sorry? But we already paid you.

>   BRENDA
>   I don't care.

>   DUSTY
>   We have the whole weekend booked.
>   We drove all the way from L.A.

Brenda sidles sideways toward the fireplace, where
the guns are.

                    BRENDA
          I don't care. You are not sleeping
          on my beds. You are not sitting on
          my couches or chairs.

                    DUSTY
          Why?

                    BRENDA
          Because you're a disgusting
          pervert? Because God know what kind of
          diseases you carry? How many reasons
          do I need, in my own goddam house?

                    DUSTY
          Okay! Fuck! Just give us our money
          back, right now, and we're gone!

Brenda plucks a RIFLE from the rack, swings it
around, points it at Dusty.

                    BRENDA
          No. You get the hell out right now.
          And I'll see you in court.

                    DUSTY
          Are you serious?

                    BRENDA
          Good luck getting your money-

> DAWN (O.S.)
> (roaring)
> AAAAAAAAUGH!!!

Suddenly, DAWN THUNDERS THROUGH THE DOORWAY. Her face HIDEOUSLY MALFORMED. Her ONE EYE BLAZING. Racing directly at Brenda.

Brenda freaks. Aims the gun at Dawn. FIRES A SHOT. Misses.

> BRENDA AND DUSTY
> (in unison)
> NO!

BRENDA FIRES AGAIN. This time, THE BULLET HITS DAWN SQUARE IN THE CHEST.

> DUSTY
> DAWN!

But DAWN JUST KEEPS COMING. Squirting BLOOD and something else. Closing in on Brenda so fast she can't even get another shot off.

> DAWN
> Fuck your gun!

DAWN PLOWS INTO BRENDA, DRIVING HER TO THE FLOOR AS THE GUN GOES FLYING.

BRENDA

Oh, God! Get offa me!

DAWN SQUEEZES BRENDA BY THE THROAT, leaning in as
Brenda's tongue protrudes, eyes bulge.

DAWN

Try praying now, you stupid cunt!

Brenda desperately RAKES HER NAILS ACROSS DAWN'S
FACE.

This UNLEASHES A TORRENT OF PUS, CASCADING DOWN
into BRENDA'S OPEN MOUTH AND EYES. She gurgles
voiceless, thrashing.

LITTLE LUMPS ERUPTING ALL OVER HER FACE AND BODY.

Meanwhile, Dusty stands, stunned. Wincing at the
stench. Not knowing what to do.

She looks at her malformed hand. SEES A TINY
FACE APPEAR IN HER PALM, on one of her throbbing
nodules.

It is DAWN'S FACE.

It SMILES at her.

DUSTY SCREAMS.

DAWN'S TINY FACE
> (with a tiny voice)
I love you.

On the floor, BRENDA FLAILS, GAGGING ON THE PUS as she's strangled. It's a hideous death, made even worse by the fact that DAWN WON'T STOP GRINNING, even as her BLOOD AND GOOP POURS OUT.

Only once BRENDA IS DEAD does Dawn relax her grip. SAGGING FORWARD. Then TOPPLING OVER.

Only then does DAISY RACE FORWARD, taking her dying lover in her arms.

DUSTY
Oh, baby-

DAWN
(chuckling)
This sure got fucked up, huh.

DUSTY
Yeah.

DAWN
I don't think we're gonna get to make our movie.

Dusty starts crying. Dawn starts laughing. Until both of them are doing both. Holding each other tight.

                    DUSTY
          This is our movie now.

                    DAWN
          Yeah.

                    DUSTY
          We're living it.

                    DAWN
          Yeah.

                    DUSTY
          Together. I swear.

                    DAWN
          I'm not dying. I'm not...

But she is. Very definitely. The POOL OF BLOOD AND
GOO spreading immensely all around them.

That's when A DOZEN MORE TINY DAWN FACES emerge
from Dusty's pustules.

And A DOZEN TINY DUSTY FACES appear all over Dawn.

All of them seeing each other, in each other.

As Dusty and Dawn LOCK EYES.

And in silent understanding, DUSTY PULLS DAWN
AROUND until Dawn's back is against Dusty's chest.
Their heads level. Both facing the same way...

...as DAWN MELTS INTO DUSTY, their TWO BODIES
TURNING INTO ONE. With A HUNDRED TINY FACES OF
EACH OTHER all over that one self.

While, beside them on the floor, DEAD BRENDA'S
CORPSE starts SQUIRTING OUT STINKLEBERRIES. The
same slimy apricot-pit-looking shit they first saw
on the hood of their car.

The new TWO-HEADED DUSTY/DAWN observes this, and
start LAUGHING.

> DAWN HEAD
> Oh, look at that shit.

> DUSTY HEAD
> What does it mean?

> DAWN HEAD
> Fuck if I know!

> DUSTY HEAD
> Aw, c'mon, my love. It means we're
> in Cancervania.

> DAWN HEAD
> Ohhhh...

>   DUSTY HEAD
> And you know what that means,
> right?

They grin at each other. Their TWO HEADS CLOSE
ENOUGH TO KISS. Tenderly. Beautifully. Which they
do.

Then pull back, with ferocious, triumphant grins.

>   DUSTY AND DAWN HEADS
>   (in unison)
> WE'RE THE QUEEN OF CANCERVANIA!

They bust up laughing, together.

>   DAWN HEAD
> Look out, assholes! There's a new
> queen in town!

>   DUSTY HEAD
> Fuck, I love a happy ending.

>   FADE TO BLACK.

ESSAYS

Intro to
HAPPINESS TIPS FOR
THE PROFOUNDLY HAUNTED

A couple years back, I was invited to participate in a collection of essays and think pieces for horror writers. Only this time, it wasn't about dispensing important writing tips like "How to Be Scary!" or "Fifty Ways to Say 'I Killed You!'".

To my delight, this was intended as a self-help book for creatives who tend to work the dark side of the street. A *Chicken Soup for the Soul* aimed at the predictable crises that come from plumbing the depths. I thought it was a great idea. And the moment I was asked, I knew exactly what I wanted to say.

It breaks my heart that the book has not, as of yet, come out. Which makes me doubly glad that I am able to include it here. Cuz I told the editor, the second I sent it in, that I would want to include this in my next collection. TA-DAAAAH!!!

And though parts of this advice are skewed toward horror writers, in particular, I'm hoping there's stuff in there that might be of use to everyone.

HAPPINESS TIPS FOR THE PROFOUNDLY HAUNTED

I don't talk about my own crushing depression much. In fact, I talk about it so rarely that most people most likely assume: 1) *I don't have any*; and 2) *I probably don't even know what the fuck depression is.*

They are, of course, mistaken. But it's completely understandable. Most of the time, I walk around in an almost ridiculously cheerful state, to the point that I'm practically the poster child for the annual "World's Happiest Horror Writers" calendar. Which, of course, does not exist.

And lemme tell you: it ain't just the extremely high quality of the medicinal weed I now legally smoke on a daily basis. Although that's definitely a contributing factor. (More on that later!)

It's about the strategies I have concocted, over the years, to keep myself from succumbing to the black abyss that continually beckons me to give up, surrender, just die and be done. An abyss that never goes away.

So when people ask me, "Why do you write about such horrible things? You seem like such a positive guy!", I just smile. Because within the question lies the answer.

And then I tell them what I'm about to tell you, as a fellow horror writer, or a reader who seeks to understand.

THE LOGIC OF DEPRESSION IN A WORLD MADE OF PAIN

The great William Goldman has a line near the beginning of his astonishing novel CONTROL that has stuck with me from the moment I first stumbled upon it. It's not a horror novel proper. But it is crawling with all the essential ingredients: violence, dread, terror, wrongness, pain.

The line is: "Life is mostly people you love and sadness."

I love this line. It crystallizes something that I think is at the heart of the human condition. Which is that *deep caring equals deep sorrow.*

Because life is often brutally and cruelly unjust. And every time cruelty or injustice happen, it puts a wound on your soul. Whether it happened directly to you or not.

Which is to say -- seen in this light -- that *depression is a natural empathetic response to being an even remotely alert and sensitive human being,* in the same way that I'd be hard-pressed to suggest that every living person doesn't have at least *some* level of PTSD. I mean, the trauma just keeps coming, right? To the point that you've barely negotiated the last one before the next one barrels in. One major signifying life crisis aside, the word "post" seems almost laughably beside the point, if not entirely redundant.

There's a cumulative weight to all that sorrow, all that damage. It can break your heart, break your back, lay you low. Make it almost impossible to get up from it, whether it hits first thing in the morning or waits till your workaday day is done before fully unleashing its payload of pain. Infecting your dreams every bit as much as it infected every second you walked around carrying it, awake.

So what do you do with it? How do you process it? How do you keep going?

As a horror writer, my answer is: you gotta find someplace to put it.

So I put it in the work.

Baby, when I write me some fucking horror, I am not kidding around. You wanna know what horror is? How bad shit gets? Well, HERE'S SOME NOW! This is what defined the splatterpunk era for me. An agenda I pursue to this day.

Horror is the genre uniquely designed to address the damage, and that's precisely what drew me to it. It was and still is my way of not just venting but *exploring and expressing that pain and terror and remorse at being unable to stop it from happening.* Except when I can.

Addressing the damage. Seeking solutions. Creating characters going through that shit, too, and letting us fictively explore ways of dealing.

There are several strains of horror-related fiction -- those now being called "weird fiction" or "cosmic horror" in particular -- that draw their enormous power from demonstrating how it feels to succumb to powerlessness. Experiencing the full fear of doom, and the absence of hope, and passing that nightmare onto us.

The braver they are, the more I love them. They nail that flavor and state of mind. They let us know that we are not alone in those crippling feelings. That we share them. THAT'S WHY WE'RE SO FUCKING DEPRESSED.

That said: much of my favorite horror fiction and film is weirdly instructional. It asks the question, "How would YOU deal with this shit, if it happened? Like, in ways that might actually work?"

And yes, it's often dialed to specific horror terms. (I can't even count the internet groups focused on how to survive a zombie apocalypse. You know. JUST IN CASE!)

But past "You got a vampire? POP A STAKE IN ITS HEART!", the best characters in the best horror stories are trying to negotiate their mental, spiritual, and emotional stakes, not to mention the survival of their bodily parts. They're being put through the wringer. And we're hoping that at least SOMEBODY rises to the occasion. Hopefully several.

We call those people heroes. Flaws and all.

Because they gave us hope that we might possibly do so, too.

I must confess to being one of those artists, by and large. Questions are great, but I'd love some fucking answers. Am not particularly interested in dropping my audience into the deepest hell, and just leaving them there. It's just another kind of self-punishing cruelty.

And in the words of hippie philosopher Alan Watts, "Once you get the message, you hang up the phone."

Insofar as I can tell, the only antidote to hopelessness is hope. And not just bullshit hope. Something that's not just symbolic, but demonstrative and actionable. Not just a theory. But a thing you can do, every day, whether the monsters are coming or not.

SO HERE'S WHAT HAPPENED TO ME

My last full nervous breakdown -- of which I'd had several -- was in 1993, right after Skipp & Spector broke up, and my life collapsed entirely. My family. My self-esteem. Everything I thought I was, and defined myself by, caved in.

I could not possibly have hated myself more. And spent much of the following year-anna-half curled up in a fetal ball, screaming, in a shithole apartment in Los Angeles, where all my dreams had gone to die.

I screamed and screamed. I felt sooooo sorry for my neighbors, who I was mostly so nice as pie with that they forgave my ululating wails of torment as best they could. They knew how far my stupid formerly New York Times bestselling ass had fallen. Were pretty sure that I meant well. And living in Hollywood, all had pains of their own. They knew from damage and broken dreams.

My biggest shame was feeling how completely I'd failed everybody I loved, by failing myself. Every time I made anyone else feel my pain, I felt like I'd just added more pain to the world, without giving anything back.

This was a clearly untenable position. And seeing no answer, I daily prayed for death. "Please," I urged God or whatever, "just let this just be over."

I wasn't gonna kill myself overtly, cuz I'm just too goddam stubborn. But if God or whatever had taken me out, at any point along that stage, I theoretically would have been immensely grateful. An end to the pain at last. Maybe infinite blackness. Or perhaps a fresh start in my soul's evolution. Either way sounded good to me.

The funny thing was: I just kept not dying.

Like maybe I wasn't done yet.

And then one day -- long story short -- I woke up and turned on KCRW, one of the finest radio stations in God's domain. And Chris Douridas, host of *Morning Becomes Eclectic*, just happened to feature an interview and live performance with Bjork. One of my favorite living artists. And someone who seemed to be radiating pure life-engaging light, at that juncture in her journey.

She played a lot of amazing music. And said a lot of amazing things. But the one thing she said that literally turned my life around was this:

"Happiness, too," and I paraphrase here, "is possible. It's a thing we can learn how to do. And if we put as much time into learning how to be happy as we do into our relationships, or our job, or career, or our favorite sports club, we might get pretty good at it."

Swear to God, that was the moment my life changed.

Here I was, begging for death to claim me. But frankly, I was tired of lying around, waiting for death. If I had to keep living, I needed a really good reason.

And it wasn't like I didn't know what happiness might feel like. I felt happiness every time I heard one of her fucking songs. I wouldn't even know what depression or sorrow were if I hadn't loved enough to feel the spark of genuine happiness rise up and sweetly bite me on the ass a trillion times.

It was at precisely that point that I decided to figure out how happiness works. And began training like a bodybuilder, or a martial artist, to develop the skills that might take me there.

How to weaponize joy, into a weapon that hurts no one.

So here are my important safety tips!

THE ANATOMY OF HAPPINESS FOR THE HAUNTED

First, let us define our terms, because everybody's got their own ideas as to what "happiness" might mean.

Some define it in terms of goals, as in, "If I finish/sell this story, or book, or script, that would make me really happy." Or, "If he/she/they fell in love with me, I would be soooo happy." Maybe it's a job. Maybe it's a new apartment or house, maybe in that new town of their dreams. Maybe it's curing cancer (for those of you who both write horror *and* are working on that cancer cure!).

Those all sound fine and dandy, and I wish you luck with each! The big thing is, you gotta understand that these are all *conditional* happinesses, on the deferred payment plan, dependent entirely on the success of your endeavor. If they happen, you presume a rush of happy will ensue. And you might be right. Or you might be wrong.

One thing I've noticed, in my long-ass life of accomplishments and failures, is that these goal-oriented hopes for satisfaction don't always feel the way you thought they would. The first time I made a major book deal, I absolutely jumped up and down, and threw a party in my head, going, "WOOOOOO!!!" But after the rush wore off, I found myself thinking, "You just got a major book deal. So why are you still SO SAD?"

And, of course, as everybody knows, nothing makes you happier than *when shit totally doesn't go your way*. The piece doesn't sell. They will never fall in love with you. The apartment falls through. People keep dying of cancer.

So much as I advocate for proactively going after the things you think might make you happy, I recommend you do not hang your hat or shingle there. Mostly because you're banking entirely on shit that's almost completely out of your control. Your happiness is dependent on the decisions of others, who may not be inclined to grant it to you, or see it as their problem to fix.

Even more, it positions happiness as *forever something in the future*. Like happiness is some prize you have to wrest from the universe, like an underdog defeating the returning champion (known as "Unhappiness"). And even if you win, Unhappiness will demand a rematch. And this game goes on forever.

Does that sound like fun to you?

No wonder, then, that many people strongly believe that happiness is bullshit. A cheesy Smiley Face emoji. A lie we tell ourselves, because we're weak and foolish, just another sucker chasing a stick that doesn't even actually exist, and mocks us every step of the way.

We'll never be rich. No one will ever love us. We'll never live anywhere we actually want to be, or have anything we want to have. Down and down into the abyss, forever.

I can't argue with this feeling, because I know it all too well. And when we're in the grip of it, it seems like the only honest and sane response to this horrible, horrible world. Even though we generally feel completely insane, while we're thinking and feeling it.

The one thing I *can* say, however, is that you ain't gonna find happiness that way.

So now let's talk about what happiness IS, in terms of my understanding.

I want to suggest that happiness is the state of joy you experience when you're simply glad to be alive, and aware, and here. Not just okay. Not just making do. And definitely not just spiraling down the wormhole, screaming.

Happiness, for me, is that moment where I catch myself smiling without thinking, without premeditation or purpose. The smile that comes up all by itself. Sneaks up and surprises me by going, "HEY! You feel good right now, baby! DOESN'T THAT FEEL NICE?"

It may be the sun, slicing down through the clouds, and warming you when you were chilled or lightless. It might be a cloud, blocking the sun from overheating you or burning your eyes. It might be the way the light refracts through the glass on your table, the beauty of the shadow on the wall. It might be the wag of the tail of the dog. The laugh of a friend. Or the genuine smile of somebody else, just passing by.

Any kind of enduring happiness is made of a trillion things that just happen, as life keeps happening. But what distinguishes those things is that a little spark ignites in your soul. It says *this is good.* It says *this is beautiful.* It says *this makes me glad I was here to experience this.*

Life is full of a trillion of these teensy incidences. They are everywhere you look, if you know how to see them.

Which brings me to…

1) LEARN HOW TO RECOGNIZE HAPPINESS, WHEN IT HITS YOU

You know when you feel it, no matter how blunted or resistant to it you may be. Run with that. Let yourself feel it. Let yourself be glad, for a second. Cherish that moment, fleeting as it may be. That is how you open the door to...

2) CULTIVATING YOUR CAPACITY FOR HAPPINESS

Cuz here's the thing. *It's hard to be happy if you don't know how.* But you DO know how. You're probably just not doing it enough. It may seem frivolous. It may seem like a distraction. But it isn't.

Most of us have deep wells and reservoirs of pain. That's already more than taken care of. But what we need to carve within ourselves is a well of joy, *a sense of well-being* every bit as deep as the pain. The deeper we dig it, the more room for it we have. And the more chance they have to balance each other out.

To use an alternate metaphor: we all know how dark shit gets. There is no bottom to how far we can fall. One trap door after another, opening. So that every time you think you hit the bottom, the floor caves in, to an even deeper darkness.

But the fact of the fucking matter is: if there is no bottom, then THERE IS NO TOP. Which means that the light, too, goes on forever. Whether you're religiously/spiritually inclined or not, the basic physics of the situation imply that without up, there is no down.

And beyond that binary breakdown is the unified field illustrated by the Tao, and its Yin/Yang symbol. A circle, half-white and half-black. Each containing the seed of the other. If the white gets too white, the seed of black blossoms. If the black overwhelms, the seed of light blooms. In either case, in the end, BALANCE IS

ACHIEVED. The Universe, going on and on.

Once you pinpoint the shit that actually makes you happy, LEAN INTO THAT SHIT! So that everything that *doesn't* make you happy is, in fact, the distraction, from the state you actually hope to achieve.

Notice the light. Notice the shadows. Notice the tail wag, and laughter, and smiles. Notice the spark that goes off within you, every time that happens. And cultivate that spark.

Like Bjork said: the more effort we put into figuring out what makes us happy, and then DOING THOSE THINGS, and maintaining that awareness, the better at it we're liable to get.

3) DO THINGS THAT MAKE YOU GENUINELY HAPPY.

This harkens back to the goal-oriented shit I was talking about earlier. Only without leaning on the goals.

You wanna write that thing? GO WRITE THAT THING. But do it not in hopes of future reward, but for the singular pleasure of the doing itself. Maybe people will like it. Maybe they won't. That's not your fucking problem.

And if writing the deepest, darkest thing in the history of the universe somehow lightens your load with its expression, and ignites that spark within you, then that is a fucking win.

The same goes with love. You want somebody to love you? AIM SOME FUCKING HAPPINESS AT THEM. It may not get you what you think you wanted, but it will most definitely give them the warmest and brightest and best you have to offer, without asking anything of them. Which is a very nice thing to do.

And while we're on the subject....

4) BE NICE TO YOURSELF.

I know this is one of the hardest things, for almost everyone. But is also the most important, if you want anything that's any good to pass along to anyone else.

In my experience, we treat ourselves worse than we would ever treat anyone else. And if we're mistreating others, it's probably because of how much we hate ourselves. Even the most narcissistic and abusive of us are just taking out on others what we most hate in ourselves.

So my advice is: treat yourself the way you'd treat somebody you really love, at your absolute best. Thank yourself when you do right. Hug and forgive yourself when you do wrong. Accept yourself for who you are. Ever mindful of that spark at your core.

The biggest obstacle most of us have is the impulse to beat the shit out of ourselves. Letting our self-loathing take the wheel, while our finest selves cower in the back seat, trembling.

That is no fucking way to live. But that hasn't stopped us before, and won't stop us again, until we just stop fucking doing it.

That means you don't get to call yourself "stupid" anymore. You don't get to say "You're an idiot", or "You're a moron", or "You're worthless: or "You suck." Personally, I don't let *anyone* talk to me like that. And I don't talk like that to anyone else, either. So why I would I let myself do it to myself?

My advice is to treat yourself like the best friend you're stuck inside the skin of. Make best friends with yourself. Recognize your flaws, but treat yourself with the kind of kindness and compassion you hope anybody else might grace you with.

The more you ignite your own spark, the more you have to offer to anyone else.

5) PUT THAT DARK SHIT IN THE WORK INSTEAD

Your friends and loved ones (and lemme be clear: if you have a readership that cares about your work, they will perceive themselves as friends and loved ones, because you will have connected in ways that count) WANT you to address your deepest demons, and be honest every speck of the way.

What they *don't* want is for you to lay your bullshit on them in cruel and hurtful ways. There's no happiness down that path.

The better you treat other people, the more happy you are likely to be.

Happiness feeds itself, much as unhappiness and depression do. They do so with repetition.

If you can put all that darkness in the art, you may find yourself relieved of the need to punish others in your personal life, and find yourself rewarded by others who appreciate your courage and compassion. Are inspired by it. And maybe even do so, themselves.

Final note on this subject: there are few things that make me happier than *making other people happy*. That's why so many religions talk about the value of being of service to others. The more joy you spread, the more of it there is. That shit is contagious. PASS IT ON!

In conclusion: this is a path, should you choose to choose it. Speaking personally, all I can say is that I've become a substantially happier person than I'd ever thought I'd ever be.

I know a lot of horror people who have worked out their damage through their work, and become happier, more balanced, and better people by following steps similar to these.

Every time we shine the light, we make the world a brighter and happier place.

It may not be the cure for depression. (Did I mention medicinal weed?)*

But if your spark and mine connected at any point along the way, then at least you know you're not alone.

Hope you're nearly as happy to know me as I am to know you.

LOVE YOU!!!

And those are my emotional safety tips.

------

* (Because it's legal now in more than half of the United States, and I absolutely swear by it as an alternative to the zombifying effects of much Big Pharma. You just have to find the right strain that works for you, in terms of reducing things like anxiety, depression, and insomnia, as well as more physical ailments from aches and pains to the results of chemo.

That said: if you've got the drug that works for you, and weed does not, DO THAT!)

Intro to
THE ONE LONG CONVERSATION

It was only after I finished the rest of the book, and placed the pieces all in order, that I realized the one thing left unsaid, just to cap it all off.

The one last button.

Which you should totally push.

THE ONE LONG CONVERSATION

You know it when you're in it. You've been in it your whole life. It comes up when you least expect it. But when it happens, you know.

You're talking with someone, going this way or that. What happened to them today. A joke. A trauma. Quite possibly both.

And suddenly, shit got real.

Suddenly, you're talking about the meaning of life. What the point of it is. Why we're even doing this.

The world takes on a particular glow, in that moment. It's the glow of a soul, opening. The walls come down. The happy horseshit peels back. The grins grow wiser. Like, "Okay, this is you and me really talking now."

Fact is, there are a lot of other conversations along the way. Small talk. Pleasantries and politenesses. Strictly transactional discussions: at work, at home, in commerce, or wherever. Sweet talk for lovers. Shit talk. Gossip. Innuendo. Lots and lots of complaining. The occasional full-blown confrontation. And then just horsing around with friends, sharing laughs and enthusiasms for fun.

They all have their place in the scheme of things.

But they all pale beside the one long conversation.

So what distinguishes it from the rest of life's jibber-jabber, and pulls it all into focus?

It generally starts with an observation about life that cuts beneath the surface of the day-to-day. One minute, you're talking about that asshole at work, or in line at the store, or you think that you're in love with. But before you know it, you're talking about the nature of assholery, and what would make a person behave like that.

Suddenly, you're sharing your own capacity for assholism. Ruefully acknowledging your own mistakes. And instead of being judged or lectured, the person you're talking with starts admitting to their own fuck-ups and foibles as well. Putting you on an honest, level playing field.

So the one long conversation is, for starters, an honest one, with its roots in humility and a willingness to listen. If that component isn't there, it's probably not the conversation I'm discussing. Although it may be gateway-drug adjacent.

Once the microcosm has been established, the macrocosm opens wide. Talking about human nature often leads to talking about Nature itself. This can take all kinds of forms. If you're the outdoorsy type, or work the land, you may ground your insights there. If you're the sciency type, it might be medicine, or space exploration, or particle physics.

If you're politically inclined, it might go to societal trends, or economic theory. If you're a therapist, or in therapy, it might be psychology, or mental illness. If you're an artist, or a lover of art, odds are good that art is likely to come up.

And if you're a person with no interests whatsoever, you're probably not having the one long conversation. But probably also do not exist.

The point is that we're all unique people, with our unique perspectives and experiences. And in the one long conversation, we realize we're all intrinsic pieces of the infinite jigsaw puzzle that is the whole of existence.

That there is a Big Picture. And that we're all in it.

No matter how tiny in context we are.

One of the greatest things about the one long conversation is that, midway through connecting the myriad dots, we've often SOLVED ALL THE WORLD'S PROBLEMS. Which is incredibly exciting, every single time.

But then it always doubles back around to, "But what am I supposed to do about this? How am I supposed to live? What is my function on this Earth?"

Somehow, it's way easier to solve all the world's problems -- at least in theory -- than it is to solve our own. We all have organically-grown blind spots, which seem to be not a bug, but an essential feature of our design. And the less we look inward, the blinder we are.

Of course, honesty and self-awareness are not our natural default settings. They are things we grow into by degrees, if we grow into them at all. Often, if not always, propelled by outside voices and incidents that force us to take stock.

Which, theoretically, is what we get whole lives for.

That's why it's such a looooooooong conversation.

The beauty of it is that it is *a conversation*. One that runs our whole lives long. And we have it not just one time, but over and over, with different people, at various points along the way. Each of whom has their own blind spots, their own cross to bear. Their own questions. And their own insights into the you that you're sharing, and vice versa. Giving each other the perspectives we could not possibly have, until we share them.

And that is the heart of the dance.

Again: it often happens when we least expect it. But it can happen any time, with almost anyone who is willing to meet you there. And partake in it, too.

I am very lucky to have had this conversation hundreds

if not thousands of times, with far too many people to count. Best friends. Total strangers. People I didn't think I liked, but who opened themselves to me in ways that made me love them forevermore.

Sometimes I start it, because I love that conversation, and would rather have it than any other conversation in the world. Just as often, somebody else opens the door, and I happily step inside. Because there's no place I'd rather be.

When I write a book like this -- or anything else I've ever written, in any form -- it's just me adding another piece to the one conversation that matters most. Taking it as far as I can, for as long as I last. Knowing it will go on long after I'm gone.

This is how we pass the torch, keep the fire of soul alive, whether just meeting minds for a couple of minutes or lighting each other's cigarettes for a sweet all-nighter on my front porch, or wherever the wild world takes us.

Thank you for having this conversation with me. Always happy to hear your side.

Best as I can tell, we are here to enjoy each other. Appreciate each other.

And help each other grow.

Also by CLASH Books

Hexis
Charlene Elsby

Dimentia
Russell Coy

I'm From Nowhere
Lindsay Lerman

Girl Like a Bomb
Autumn Christian

Darryl
Jackie Ess

Waterfall Girls
Kimberly White

Girl in the Walls
Katy Michelle Quinn

Helena
Claire L. Smith

Cenote City
Monique Quintana

Tragedy Queens:
Stories Inspired by Lana Del Rey & Sylvia Plath
Edited by Leza Cantoral

No Name Atkins
Jerrod Schwarz

Jah Hills
Unathi Slasha

Sequelland
Jay Slayton-Joslin

Dark Moons Rising on a Starless Night
Mame Bougouma Diene

If You Died Tonight I Would Eat your Corpse
Wrath James White

Nightmares in Ecstasy
Brendan Vidito

Horror Film Poems
Christoph Paul

Goddamn Killing Machines
David Agranoff

The Mummy of Canaan
Maxwell Bowman

This is a Horror Book
Charles Austin Muir

The Very Ineffective Haunted House
Jeff Burk

He Has Many Names
Drew Chial

Zombie Punks Fuck Off
Edited by Sam Richard

CL◀SH

WE PUT THE LIT IN LITERARY

CLASHBOOKS.COM

Follow us

Twitter
IG
FB
@clashbooks

Email
clashmediabooks@gmail.com